The office grew silent as their eyes locked, each assessing the other . . .

Jan broke eye contact first and began to speak slowly, meticulously. "Mr. Toliver, I appreciate what you said at the board meeting this morning. You pay me well for what I do, but it's always nice to hear that my work is valued. Thank you for inviting me here."

"Believe me, the pleasure is all mine," he said, his eyes shining with a light Jan hadn't seen before. His look made her more uncomfortable as he continued speaking. "And since you've been sleeping with me all day . . . so to speak . . . why don't you call me Kevin."

"All right," she agreed as a flush rose to her cheeks, and she forced herself to remain calm.

"J. P. Harper, you blush wonderfully," he said softly, intimately.

SOMEDAY, SOMEWHERE

SOMEDAY, SOMEWHERE

Mary Kay McComas

PAGEANT BOOKS

PAGEANT BOOKS
225 Park Avenue South
New York, New York 10003

PAGEANT and colophon are trademarks of the publisher

Cover artwork by Franco Accornero

Printed in the U.S.A.

First Pageant Books printing: November, 1988

10 9 8 7 6 5 4 3 2 1

*This book is dedicated to
Doss, for his encouragement;
to Pete, for typing it;
and to my children, who were patient with me.*

SOMEDAY,
SOMEWHERE

Chapter One

◆ ◆ ◆

"WHAT AM I doing here?" Jan Harper had asked herself that same question at least a hundred times since she'd arrived in New York. "And where is that old poop, Toliver? I can't stand around here all day." Jan eyed what she supposed was a piece of modern art standing in the corner of the boardroom of Toliver, Inc. "And what the hell is that?" To her it looked like a collection of scrap metal welded together haphazardly with no regard to symmetry, purpose, or even pleasure to the eye.

Her own eyes were dry and scratchy from lack of sleep. Her lids felt heavy, and she was afraid to blink for fear they would remain shut. Every muscle in her tall, slim body was threat-

1

ening to go on strike if she didn't find someplace to lie down soon. Her headache had subsided to a dull throb in her temples, but her nerves were still standing on end. Jan's cool, calm front threatened to shatter into a million pieces.

The heavy oak doors of the boardroom opened finally, and Jan's eyes turned toward it, as did the other eight pairs of eyes in the room, belonging to the various heads of departments gathered there for an executive committee meeting of Toliver, Inc.

In her fatigue-induced stupor, it took several seconds for Jan to register what she saw. She'd been expecting an older man, but this was ridiculous. This man had to be over eighty if he was a day. He was shorter than Jan's five feet seven inches, and very thin. *Well, how am I going to jump all over that poor little man,* she thought with disappointment.

Her summons for a command performance at this meeting had been waiting for her the night before when she'd returned to the Western Division of Toliver, Incorporated, in Denver after two very long days of researching and visiting possible sites for the ever-expanding Toliver empire. She'd been very surprised at first, as she'd never had any contact with the hierarchy of the company before. She was an industrial site planning consultant who did most of her work for Toliver, Inc., but whose only contact was Gil Anderson, Director of Planning in Denver. He sent her reports and recommendations on to New York. Here they were considered by this executive committee, then reconsidered by the board of directors. The decision to accept or reject her recommendations came to her by reverse order through Gil.

At the moment she was more than a little disgusted with this Mr. Toliver. She'd done several projects for him and was still miffed about a particularly juicy stretch of industrial land in Arizona she found for him the previous year. She'd sent her report in, convinced that he would send her a Nobel Prize by return mail. Three weeks later she'd been informed that he had gone with his own original choice in the L.A. area. She had plotted and researched that area for him, too, but the Arizona land was cheaper and a more accessible location with equal resources. At the time she had decided he was a total fool, but, seeing him now, thought that maybe he was a little senile.

Jan's time was sorely limited at present, so she'd flown cross-country overnight to spend the day in New York discussing her latest project, which she'd submitted over a month ago. It wasn't quite the first-prize job the Arizona deal had been, but her recommendation beat the stuffings out of both of his preferred land choices. Jan was bound and determined to make him see reason this time. Then again, at his age maybe he had more money than sense.

The little man cleared his throat and spoke clearly but softly. "Ladies and gentlemen, Mr. Toliver has asked me to beg your patience. He has been detained, but plans to make his appearance as soon as possible. He indicated to me it would not be more than thirty minutes."

Looking around, Jan noticed that after their initial inspection of the little man, the others in the room had dismissed him and gone back to their own private thoughts and discussions. They took his announcement in stride and didn't seem to notice that he didn't leave the room.

He walked somewhat slowly but steadily to a small cart to the right of the large double doors. He poured a cup of coffee and placed it on a silver tray with the cream and sugar. Picking it up, he turned slowly and began walking in Jan's direction.

The closer he got, the more Jan realized her initial impression wasn't completely correct. He looked to be in his sixties and he was far from senile. His eyes, watching and assessing her in return, were a sharp, clear pewter gray. He had a thick thatch of gray hair, which was neatly groomed. The gray of his hair, the gray of his eyes, and the erect carriage of his small body all distinguished him as a man of great wisdom and knowledge.

It may have been all the years she'd spent with her own very wise grandfather that prompted Jan to instantly respect this little man, or it may have been the fact that he was also bestowing on her the first friendly smile she'd had all morning. For both reasons she smiled back.

"Ms. Harper?" he asked softly.

"Yes."

"My name is Hobbs. Mr. Toliver asked me to

make sure you were comfortable until he got here. Would you like some coffee?" he asked, offering her the tray.

She had already drunk enough coffee in her effort to stay awake and the mere smell of this rich brew almost made her nauseated, but she took the cup, saying, "Thank you, Mr. Hobbs."

"Have you had time to get settled in the hotel suite, or did you come straight from the airport?" he asked politely.

"Well, no, I . . ." Her voice trailed off as she heard her name coming from someone seated at the large oak table in the middle of the room. Glancing over, she couldn't tell at first who was speaking.

"Harper? Did you say your name was Harper?"

"Yes." She turned to a slightly overweight man on her left. He was a balding, dark-haired man with dark eyes and pinched lips. His face looked to be on the angry side with some apprehension mixed in. The combination gave Jan the feeling of being an unwelcome adversary and put her on the defensive immediately.

"J. P. Harper? From Denver?" the man continued.

"Yes," she repeated.

"What are you doing here?"

Jan almost laughed, as she had been asking herself the same question, but he had directed it at her with such hostility that she thought better of it. "I was asked to come by Mr. Toliver," she replied calmly in her low, husky voice, made huskier from lack of sleep.

"Why?" he demanded.

"I'm not sure, Mr. . . ."

"Talbet. Charles Talbet," he filled in the blank for her.

The name was familiar to Jan. Charles Talbet was vice-president of operations for Toliver, Inc. It was to him her reports and recommendations were submitted for presentation to Mr. Toliver, this committee and the board of directors. Obviously, he knew who she was.

"I'm not sure why I'm here, Mr. Talbet. I presume it has something to do with the plats I recommended for the Computer Research Center and Assembly Plant last month," she informed him. While she spoke she watched the anger in his face increase and she instinctively stood taller and straightened her tired shoulders in preparation for battle.

"That's ridiculous," he stated flatly, his voice rising angrily. "I've already presented that proposal and I've recommended the southern California site."

"The southern California site . . ." She trailed off, confused. *That* was ridiculous! The Nevada land was cheaper and larger, so both units could be built together to make it even more economical. The natural resources were perfect, not to mention the sociological makeup of the surrounding communities. Suddenly her fatigue began to dissipate, taking with it her calm, her patience, and her temper, all of which she would normally have had more control over.

She thrust out her strong, determined chin. Her moss-green eyes began to darken and snap with anger. She flipped her head to one side, tossing her shiny shoulder-length auburn hair to one side.

A wiser person would have detected these subtle changes in Jan and would have considered it a day and gone home. Mr. Talbet was not a wise man.

His eyes slowly moved down her obviously feminine form, taking in her pale pink cotton shirt with its rolled-up sleeves that fit her loosely but showed off her curves in a very appealing fashion. He glanced at the apple-green pullover sweater tied loosely around her shoulders by its sleeves then moved down her body to take in her slim waist and lean, softly rounded hips and long, firm legs wrapped in the form-fitting jeans she'd worn for comfort on the plane. He briefly noted her white running shoes, then began his slow ascent, his eyes resting on her breasts once more before he began to speak again.

"You know, *Ms.* Harper," he said snidely, emphasizing the title before her name, "the casual work atmosphere in the West may work . . . in the West, but it doesn't make much of an impression here. It's my impression that a person's personal habits reveal volumes about his . . . or her work habits."

Practically blinded by red hot anger, and with her hands fisted, she walked lithely past Hobbs and halfway down the table until she was directly opposite Charles Talbet. She slowly laid her hands, palms flat, on the table and met Talbet's gaze with her own.

"You pompous . . ." She stopped herself, thinking name-calling wouldn't be a terribly mature move, and although she had a whole list of things she'd like to call him, it would serve no purpose.

"Mr. Talbet," she started over, taking in a slow, deep breath, "I would like to apologize for my attire this morning. You might like to know, I did bring something you would have found more appropriate for this auspicious occasion, but I foolishly set my bag down in the ladies' room at the airport, and when I went to retrieve it, it was gone. The authorities at the airport advised me not to expect to see it again." She paused briefly to take another deep breath, then continued, her eyes never wavering.

"As to your insinuation that my casual attire reflects casualness in my work, I'd like you to know that I have spent the last two days crawling through courthouse records, talking to some very boring real estate agents, and slogging around in mud up to my knees, plotting lots for a floppy disk factory for this company. This is my third day without sleep, Mr. Talbet," she went on in a low, husky voice that did nothing to conceal her fury, "but I'm still strong enough to tell you I do damn good work for this company. And I'm still awake enough to see that only a fool would pick the southern California sites over the site in Nevada. Since you've already proven my point there, then I'll concede a point to you, Mr. Talbet. It is ridiculous for me to be here."

Taking one last look at an astonished Talbet, she straightened to her full height, turned on her heel, and walked briskly to the door.

Thank God for Hobbs, Kevin Toliver thought as the elevator doors swept open on the fourteenth floor and he headed for his office at a harried pace. That damned Jeff Manning can talk your face off.

The early morning breakfast meeting had been Manning's idea of a good time to discuss the Toliver purchase of a Manning subsidiary. Manning was a tough, shrewd businessman and Kevin respected him for that, but the man could talk forever on any given subject and now Kevin was late for his own executive board metting.

It was a little embarrassing, especially since he'd wanted to make an impression on J. P. Harper this morning. With any luck at all today, he'd convince Harper to come to work for him permanently and take Talbet's place on the board. Last week when he had discovered what Talbet was doing, he'd almost fired him on the spot. After careful consideration, and with Hobbs's restraining hand on his shoulder, he had decided to give the man a chance to retire gracefully. Talbet was basically a good man and had served the company well for twelve years. Kevin had been vaguely aware of some domestic problems in Talbet's life lately, and he was sorry they had gotten so far out of hand, but dishonesty was dishonesty, and Talbet had cost the company millions of dollars last year with the Arizona proposal he had concealed.

This Harper guy did great work. He'd definitely be an asset. To top it off, when Kevin read over Harper's employment record, he'd discovered that J. P. Harper had worked his way rapidly through the ranks at Manning Industries and had left the position of vice-president of operations there two years before to strike out on his own as an industrial site planning consultant.

This morning when Kevin had mentioned to Jeff Manning that he was going to try to get J. P. Harper for the same position on his own board, Manning had appeared startled, then somewhat thoughtful as he'd said, "Well, I never had any complaints about the kid's work. The move back to New York will be your biggest obstacle."

"I'll just have to make him an offer he can't refuse," Kevin decided.

Approaching the boardroom, Kevin noticed that the doors had been left wide open. As he slowed his pace to glance into the room, he saw that everyone's attention was riveted to the far wall. There, standing beside Hobbs, was an incredibly lovely sight to behold at this time of morning—actually, she'd be a pleasure to look at any time of the day.

The woman had reddish-brown hair the color of chestnuts. Even under the concealed fluorescent lighting it sent off sparks of copper and gold. He couldn't see what color her eyes were, but they were large and expressive. She looked tired, and angry about something. His eyes slid down her figure of soft curves and swells, and even dressed in jeans—or maybe because of the jeans—he felt his breath catch in his throat.

Who was she? Maybe Harper's wife or girl-friend? The thought that she might belong to Harper sent a sudden flash of disappointment through him. Oh, he'd known and had his share of beautiful women, but this one was exquisite and, oddly enough, it rankled him to think that he wouldn't be able to touch her because she belonged to someone else.

He glanced around the room for Harper. The only unfamiliar face in the room was hers.

With eyes squinted in speculation, he continued on down the hall to his office. After a brief good morning to his secretary, Katherine, Kevin was pushing aside papers on his desk until he came up with the file he was looking for. There it was. "J. P. Harper. Industrial site planning consultant. Denver. Last employed at Manning Industries as . . ." Yes, yes, he knew all that.

Flipping to the back pages of the file, he read, "Janelle Patrice Harper. Female. Twenty-seven. Single."

He shook his head in amusement.

With a light step and an exciting sense of anticipation he gathered up the rest of the materials he needed and set off back to the boardroom, his secretary in tow.

* * *

A normally easygoing, relaxed Jan could remember only one other time in her life when
she'd been this angry. Two years ago, here in
New York, she had raged with anger and pain
and frustration at her father, whom she had
once loved very much. Just recalling that day
brought back the disappointment and disgust
she felt for him in wave after wave of intense
pain.

The memory helped to fuel the anger she felt
for that pompous Talbet. Her brisk pace had
picked up the momentum of a locomotive by the
time she reached the boardroom doors. Still
blind with fury, she nearly knocked herself out
cold when she collided full force with what she
thought was a wall.

Dizzy and winded from the force of the impact, Jan was stunned when two large hands
grabbed her upper arms as her knees buckled
under her. Gradually things began to register in
Jan's overused head. The wall *smelled* good; it
was warm too. This wall was wearing a blue
shirt. Lifting her head, her eyes slowly, numbly,
looked up a good six or seven inches and fixed
on a pair of the bluest eyes she'd ever seen. They
were the same color as the sky on a clear summer afternoon, and just as warm. She felt her
body go from shocked rigid to stunned limp and
yet still felt secure in the protective embrace.

His eyes were so close, she could see little gray
streaks of color radiating out from the pupils,
and she vaguely wondered if they changed color

with their owner's mood. She could feel a warm, moist breath on her face. She stared for what seemed like a long time before her eyes shifted down to the mouth that was spread in a warm, friendly grin, which she instantly decided went very well with the eyes. The lips looked soft, yet malapert over even white teeth, and the full lower lip had a decided sensual appeal to it. Darting back to the eyes, Jan noticed they had taken on a teasing, amused twinkle.

A queer feeling passed through her as the masculine chest rumbled against her breasts and the mouth opened to emit a low, throaty chuckle. The man breathed a low, raspy "Hello," and the spell was instantly broken.

A warm flush of embarrassment throbbed in her cheeks. Slowly Jan tested her legs and, finding them weight-bearing, she slowly disengaged herself from the man's embrace.

"J. P. Harper?" he asked, his voice a deep, soft timbre that warmed the insides of her bones.

She nodded her response.

"I'm Kevin Toliver. Thank you for coming today. I hope I haven't disrupted your schedule too much. I know it was pretty last-minute of me, but I didn't see your report until late last week," he said with a pointed glance at Talbet, who began to look anxious and pale, "and I wanted you here when we discussed it at this meeting."

As he talked, he had been gently leading Jan down the table to an empty chair just past but facing Talbet. He offered her a chair, and when she was safely seated, he returned to the head of

the table near the door and took his rightful position.

Jan dragged her eyes off him and looked down
at her hands, which were clasped gently in her
lap. She knew if she kept staring at him, she'd
look like a starry-eyed teenager, or worse yet,
she might start to drool. More embarrassment
she didn't need. *Concentrate, Jan! Stradford
Boarding School. Poise and deportment. Deep
breath. Head high. Calm features. You can do it!*

Obviously not as shaken by their collision as
she was, Kevin Toliver had opened his meeting
and was rapidly clearing away subjects on the
agenda. "You all have copies in front of you of
Ms. Harper's report on the possible sites for our
new computer research center and for the computer assembly factory," she heard him say, and
finally, gratefully, the fog in her head started to
lift and Jan's thoughts began to clear.

"I'm not sure how it was overlooked at the
first discussion," he went on to say, "but on the
basis of this report, I think we should do some
reconsidering on our choice of project sites."

Jan glanced at Charles Talbet. His face was
very pale and his eyes were darting from one
member of the board to the next. A film of perspiration had formed on his upper lip and balding forehead. Jan debated the possibility that
maybe Talbet had been filing her reports without even presenting them and that's why none of
her recommendations had come to light. But
why? Her newfound suspicion coiled in her
stomach like a snake.

"Ms. Harper?" Kevin Toliver was calling from the other end of the table.

"Yes? I'm sorry," she apologized for her obvious lack of attention.

"I was saying that I for one recognized this as an excellent piece of work. I want to thank you for your efforts on this project as well as on the others, including the one for the Arizona site last year," he complimented her, gratitude in his intense gaze.

"You're welcome," she said softly.

"Combining the two projects on one site will be extremely cost efficient. . . ."

He continued to speak, and Jan continued to draw in the warmth from his voice, but she lost track of the words and their meaning. As she leaned back in the comfortable chair, she thought, *So that's what this is all about. He dragged me all the way to New York to thank me for doing my job. Seems a little extreme; he could have sent me a letter, or called. Still it is awfully nice. . . .*

From the other end of the table Kevin continued down the agenda, stealing frequent glances at J. P. Harper. The little vixen was actually falling asleep in the middle of his board meeting. He watched as she snuggled back into the soft green leather chair and got comfortable. He saw her eyelids start to get heavy and droop and applauded the valiant effort she made to keep them open, then smiled inside when her head bobbed to one side and didn't bounce back up again.

When her soft rosy lips fell open and a quiet little snore escaped, he chuckled out loud and held up his hands to stop the meeting.

"Katherine, gentlemen, will you excuse me just a few minutes? Watching her is driving me crazy," he said with a low laugh.

He got up and walked down to Jan's chair, pulling it out gently so as not to wake her. Gently he slid his arms behind her back and under her knees, and brought her up to his chest. She was surprisingly light and she felt good in his arms.

As he walked toward his office with Jan held tightly to his chest, her head lolled onto his shoulder and fit neatly under his chin. She sighed in her sleep and he felt her breath through the heavy cloth of his shirt. A warmth spread through his veins as Kevin again decided that he was very glad that J. P. Harper wasn't the man he'd thought she was.

Chapter Two

◆ ◆ ◆

KEVIN HAD GONE back to the boardroom and
had sat out the meeting only to return to his office, where he had been at his desk for the past
five hours trying desperately to get some work
done. He couldn't remember ever having been
so distracted. He had already read over several
reports two or three times each before he'd felt
able to understand them enough to responsibly
initial his satisfaction with them.

Then again, he couldn't ever remember having enjoyed a distraction more. It came in the
form of the beautiful woman sleeping on his
couch directly across the room from him.

He had lost count of the times he'd found himself just sitting, with his elbows on the desk, the
heels of his hands supporting his chin, and
watching her sleep, like he was now. Oddly, he
found that he was truly enjoying it.

When she mumbled softly in her sleep, Kevin
leaned closer to make out what she was saying.
When she sighed and cuddled deeper into the
pillow under her head, he thought of how he'd

like to make her sigh like that and have her cuddle closer to him. When she unconsciously stuck the tip of her pink tongue out and wet her soft, rosy lips, he fantasized about licking her lips with his own tongue, and groaned inwardly. Then, when she tossed herself over onto her side, and the rounded curves of her buttocks faced him, his hands began to shake with his effort to control the throbbing in the lower half of his body. He quickly and quietly left the room in search of a cup of coffee, and to make a very necessary phone call.

"I owe you one, Manning," Kevin threatened benignly several minutes later. "When you recommended J. P. Harper as a planning consultant, you could have just mentioned in passing that he was a she . . . and a beautiful she at that. I could have looked like a huge fool at that meeting this morning."

"You mean you didn't?" Manning asked, sounding disappointed before he released a low, throaty chuckle. "I swear, boy, you're getting quicker every year. It's getting harder and harder to pull the wool over your eyes. And here I've been waiting for more than a year now for you to meet up with her face-to-face. You're no fun anymore, Toliver."

"So how come I still feel like I'm being set up for something?" Kevin asked warily.

"Tell me, have you stumbled across the offer she can't refuse yet?" Manning wondered, ignoring Kevin's suspicions.

Smiling, and recalling the sleeping form on the couch in his office, Kevin replied, "Actually, we haven't had much of an opportunity to discuss it. Got any suggestions?"

"If I did, she'd still be working for me," was his derisive answer. "I'm the last man in New York to ask for advice on women, Toliver, and you know it."

Kevin was silent for a moment, his heart going out to the man on the other end of the line. Jeff Manning did, indeed, have lousy luck with the women in his life. A widower, and later a divorcé, Manning had often spoken of his late first wife in tones that exposed his everlasting, deep love for her, his loneliness, and his sorrow. There was a daughter, too, but his friend rarely spoke of her. When he did, it was with frustration and grave remorse. Apparently Jeff Manning, loving and adoring his daughter like any man would, made several well-intentioned but miscalculated judgment calls affecting her life, as every man has at one time or another during fatherhood. On the few occasions he'd discussed it with Kevin, Jeff had openly admitted to hurting his daughter and understanding her resentment, but he'd never been able to hide that he was also racked with pain by her refusal to have anything to do with him even long enough for him to explain and apologize.

"Your daughter still won't answer your calls?" Kevin stated more than questioned.

"No."

"How can she be so coldhearted?"

"She's not. She's just the opposite, in fact. But I hurt her—more than once. She's just protecting herself," Manning defended his daughter.

"At your expense."

"I can afford it a little longer. She'll come around one day," Manning stated firmly, but Kevin could hear the hope and desperation in his tone. "In the meantime, use your best instincts on J. P. Harper. As far as I've seen, they've never failed you before."

When Kevin returned to his office, he found Jan lying on her back with both arms flung carelessly over her head. He sat for what seemed like hours just watching her firm, round breasts rise and fall with her respiration. He was indeed having an enjoyable day.

She had since rolled back to her side, facing him, and he had completely given up any attempt at finishing his work. He sat quietly and watched her sleep.

Vaguely, Jan became aware of reality as it worked its way through the mists of her consciousness. She felt warm and comfortable. She wasn't sure where she was, but she thought she wouldn't mind staying for a while.

She was very content in her sleep-induced stupor, very content indeed, except for that smell that would occasionally drift past her nose. It was a disturbing, spicy smell, not unpleasant in itself, but it brought back elusive memories. Confusion disturbed her tranquility.

She heard someone gently clear his throat.

Her eyes shot open and made direct contact with a pair of clear blue ones that were very familiar. In fact, she thought she'd just been dreaming about them. They were smiling at her with kind amusement. Funny, that's not how they had looked in her dream.

Her eyes snapped shut again as reality hit her in the face like a fist. Oh, God, it was Kevin Toliver. "I'm so embarrassed," she groaned, not realizing she had spoken out loud.

"Please don't be," he said casually, leaving his desk and coming over to squat down beside the couch next to her. "Hobbs explained what happened before I got to the meeting. I feel like the one who should apologize. I had no idea what kind of schedule you had been keeping when I had my secretary call and ask you here. And if I'd been on time, you wouldn't have had to deal with Talbet. I truly am sorry . . . but Hobbs said you did a superior job of making Talbet look the fool he really is," he finished on an amused note.

The incident washed back to her with shameful clarity. She raised a hand and rubbed her brow several times, as if the memories were causing her head to ache. Then she let her hand drop to the couch. She opened her eyes and looked at Kevin. He could see the shame and self-disgust in her eyes.

"No," she said softly, shaking her head, "I shouldn't have done that. I could have handled it much better. Poor Mr. Hobbs must think I'm a shrew."

"No, he doesn't," he assured her. "He thinks you work too hard. So do I, for that matter. Do you often go days at a time without sleep like this? Have you thought of getting some help?"

Jan could see the concern on his face and thought it was very nice of him to worry about her. She smiled at him.

"I'm not that overworked, Mr. Toliver," she explained. "I was in a hurry to get home from this last trip. I decided that instead of spending the night in Seattle, I'd go on to Portland Monday night and get an early start Tuesday. I wanted to catch an earlier flight home Tuesday afternoon. As it turned out, when I got to Portland, I couldn't find a place near the airport to stay, so I thought I'd forgo the sleep, get my work done, go home to Denver, and get rested there. Needless to say, I hadn't planned on your invitation."

"So you took the red-eye out of Denver last night to be here on time this morning, right?" he finished for her.

"Right," she said with a rueful grin.

Kevin liked it when she smiled; she had a small dimple in her left cheek that was very appealing. "And you don't sleep on airlines, right?" he guessed with a smile.

Chuckling, she sat up and put her feet on the floor. "Right," she repeated. "It's silly, I know, but staying awake somehow makes me feel like I have a little more control over my life up there."

He had been watching her closely while she spoke. She had a low, husky voice that he found extremely sexy. Her eyes were a forest green, and he got the impression that they were truly the windows to her soul. They were quick and intelligent and revealed her thoughts and feelings. At the moment he could see she was still very uncomfortable in her present situation, and she was going to bolt.

"Ms. Harper . . ."

"Mr. Toliver . . ."

They spoke simultaneously, then smiled at each other. The room grew silent as their eyes locked, each assessing the other as if what was said next would be crucial to whatever kind of relationship they would have from that point on.

Jan broke eye contact first and began to speak slowly, meticulously. "Mr. Toliver, I appreciate what you said at the meeting this morning. You pay me well for what I do, but it's always nice to hear that my work is valued. Thank you for inviting me here."

"Believe me, the pleasure is all mine," he said, his eyes shining with a light Jan hadn't seen before. His look made her more uncomfortable as he continued speaking. "And since you've been sleeping with me all day . . . so to speak . . . why don't you call me Kevin."

"All right," she agreed as a flush rose to her cheeks, and she forced herself to remain calm.

"J. P. Harper, you blush wonderfully," he said softly, intimately.

Completely flustered, Jan turned her eyes from his and glanced nervously at her watch in a desperate attempt to find a subject that would neutralize his topic of conversation.

"Good Lord. It's nearly six." She was extremely dismayed. "I have to go. I've already missed the first plane."

She was on her feet and halfway to the door when she stopped and spun around, thrusting her hand in his direction.

"It's been nice meeting you, Mr. . . . ah . . . Kevin. Thank you again."

He had taken her hand, but rather than release it when she finished speaking, he retained it in his firm clasp and covered the back of her hand with his other one. Shaking his head slowly, he asked, "What's your hurry? I'm sorry if I upset you when I teased you about your blushing, but . . ."

"No, no. That's not it at all," she broke in distractedly. "I really do have to catch the next plane out of here. I only came for the meeting. I'm sorry to rush like this, but I can't stay. I have to get home."

Worry lines creased Kevin's face, and the muscles in his chest began to constrict.

"Are you eager to get back to *someone* at home?" he asked, his throat tight.

She studied his handsome features, memorizing the details so as to recall them at a future date—the exquisite blue eyes trimmed with thick, dark lashes, the straight nose and lean cheeks, the firm, square chin beneath the sensuous curve of his lower lip, and the thick, dark hair that was not quite black but very dark brown.

Kevin Toliver made a picture to cherish. When it occurred to Jan that she'd probably never see him again, she experienced a disappointed that was almost tangible.

Impulsively her hand reached out to touch his cheek, but she caught herself and lowered both her hand and her eyes. "Yes, I guess you could say I'm eager to get home to someone," she said in a low voice.

A man, Kevin thought, and spoke the words at the same time, feeling resentful and foolish.

Hearing the disappointment in his voice that matched her own, Jan felt strangely happy. She flashed him a breathtaking smile that sent lights flashing in her eyes and said, "Two men."

Kevin had had better days than this. He felt surly and was ready to pick a fight with any likely candidate who crossed his path. He refused to acknowledge that his present disposition could have anything to do with jealousy, but pictures of that woman's face lighting up with joy and happiness when she had stated that she had two men waiting for her kept creeping back into his mind. The picture was followed by a heavy feeling in his chest.

Collecting his thoughts to the matter at hand, he determined that it didn't matter if she had fifty men in Denver holding their breath for their chance at her, he still wanted her on the board at Toliver, Inc. She had run off so fast yesterday, he hadn't even gotten a chance to try to persuade her into at least thinking about the position.

During a restless night haunted by the memory of her eyes, Kevin reviewed his earlier fantasies and debated various tactics of approach to convince her to accept a position in New York. Finally, Kevin had fallen asleep on what he considered a plausible plan of attack. He rose early, making several phone calls before his shower and breakfast. Two hours in the office caught him up on the immediate business and left his calendar open till Monday morning. Hobbs and his suitcase were waiting at the airport when he got there.

He pulled the rental car over to the side of the road and reached for the handwritten directions he'd gotten from Gil Anderson in the Denver office a little over an hour before.

He had traveled the twenty-six miles from Denver to Boulder with no problems. The turn west out of Boulder had been well marked, as had the road going north into Roosevelt National Forest. But there were fewer and fewer markers now—and fewer towns or even isolated buildings.

Good Lord, do people really live in a place called Pleasant Valley, Colorado? It seemed incredible to Kevin. It was like something out of the Dick-and-Jane-and-Spot-and-Puff-who-live-on-Maple-Street books he'd read as a kid.

These directions were incredible, too, he thought. "When you see the marker indicating

Pleasant Valley is two miles up the road, slow down and watch for a road off to the left. The road is marked by an old tree stump with a clay pot of geraniums on it." Kevin cast his eyes skyward, then continued to read. "The road goes uphill, then downhill, and turns sharply to the right. Go up the last hill and the first left is Jan's driveway. Follow it up to the cabins."

Jan. Kevin had been wondering if people called her J.P. or Janelle. Jan suited her.

He continued to drive and watch for landmarks while thoughts of Jan danced through his mind. He hadn't really placed her in this environment yet. Even dressed in jeans, she had seemed to belong in New York. She had an air of sophistication in the way she walked and held her head. Even under yesterday's circumstances, the moments when she had revealed her vulnerability were few and fleeting. Reading her reports and listening to Hobbs's account of her confrontation with Talbet, Kevin had envisioned her living the life of a modern, liberated businesswoman. He pictured her in a condominium in the more stylish districts of Denver. The thought of Jan in the wilderness on the side of a mountain outside a small town called Pleasant Valley had never occurred to him.

Having turned left into what was supposed to be Jan's driveway, Kevin found the road unrelated to its definition. It climbed at a near forty-degree angle and was full of potholes the size of bathtubs. When the rental car bounced violently over one of these yawning gaps in the road and sounds of scraping and bumping came from beneath the car, Kevin pulled over as far as he could and decided to walk the rest of the way.

Although it was late June, he noticed that it had cooled down perceptively in the late afternoon. Walking along with his hands in his pockets, he started taking in lots of other things too. The farther he went up the road, the greater was the span of the vista below him. And it was magnificent. For as far as his eyes could see, the land curved and dipped, swung up again, only to peak and slope off. Below the timberline, thick stands of Ponderosa pines, blue spruce, and aspen thrived on this side of the mountain. Here in the first wave of the Rocky Mountains to rise from the central Great Plains, Kevin could see the snow-crowned summits far above and way beyond where he stood. They were rough, spectacular, and noble. They were awe-inspiring and took Kevin's breath away.

Then again, maybe it was the uphill climb that was taking his breath away. Kevin considered himself physically fit; he exercised, playing racquetball three days a week and working with weights the other two. On most weekends he went to Southampton to his boat, but he'd never tried mountain climbing before and he was feeling the strain. It scratched his ego to think Jan ran tame all over this mountain and probably never got winded.

Although he'd been looking for them, he was

surprised when two log cabins appeared before him. They were situated on what appeared to be the only semi-level surface on this side of the mountain. Nestled in among the towering trees, they looked cozy and safe.

The cabins were spaced about a hundred feet apart and were almost identical. The structure on the right was slightly larger with a recent addition. One large room had been added to the side of the house. The logs were a good match but weren't as weathered as the rest of the house.

Drawing closer, he noted telephone and electrical power wires leading to both houses and curtains in the windows. A TV antenna dispelled the first impression of rustic authenticity. Kevin looked around for a small building with a crescent moon on the door and was relieved to find that Jan also had indoor plumbing.

Parked between the two houses was a very practical-looking Bronco with four-wheel drive. A necessity up here, Kevin suspected. Then his eyes caught sight of the vehicle in front of it. A topless jeep with a roll bar, painted fire-engine red. On the side, in bold white letters, read: JAN'S RENEGADE.

If the Renegade was Jan's, the Bronco must belong to one of her gentlemen friends, Kevin thought, feeling uneasy. He didn't want to walk into any sticky situations. On the other hand, he wasn't here for Jan's body; he wanted her mind. The guy would just have to understand.

Fleetingly, he wondered who the other cabin belonged to and which one was Jan's when he heard a woman shout through the window of the smaller cabin.

"Dammit, Jan! Get out of bed. I'm leaving now, so it's the last time I'll be calling."

Kevin came to a halt ten yards from the front porch of the smaller cabin, when he heard a low growl and something bang and clang in the larger cabin.

He was looking from one cabin to the other in indecision, when the door of the smaller opened and a middle-aged woman came out. Her wavy hair was dark, heavily streaked with silver, and was cut close around her face. She wore large round purple plastic eyeglasses and a plain sleeveless dress cinched at a thick but not obese waist. Matronly was how Kevin would describe her.

While he was assessing her, the woman stared back at him with open curiosity. Recalling his manners, Kevin cleared his throat and slapped a friendly smile on his face.

"Good afternoon," he started, "does Jan Harper live here?"

"Yes," she replied in a polite but reserved voice.

"Oh, good," he said, the relief obvious in his voice. "I'm Kevin Toliver. Would it be possible to speak to her? I think she's expecting me."

"If she's expecting you, that'll be news to both of us," the woman said dubiously.

"I sent a telegram," Kevin explained, beginning to feel a little uncomfortable.

The woman had come down the steps and was walking toward him. She came to a halt in front of him and peered into his eyes. "You're the one from New York. The one with the gorgeous blue eyes," she stated without preamble, almost as if she were speaking to herself.

"Did Jan say that?" Hope sprang in his chest, and the genuine grin on his face radiated it.

"Yes, she did, but she's not going to be too happy to see you here. She said she made a fool of herself yesterday and didn't know what she'd do if she ever had to face you again. Apparently she wasn't herself after all that traveling. She doesn't like feeling like a fool," the woman stated without any coaxing.

This woman could be a fountain of information in the right hands, Kevin speculated, but before he could speak, the woman continued.

"I have to go, but you can go in and wait for her to get up if you want to." She motioned with her head to the larger cabin, then turned toward the cars to leave before glancing back to add, "I guess I should warn you not to talk to her till after she's had her shower. She doesn't come awake quickly and she's been known to do some strange things while she's still half asleep. It's left over from her New York days. Even the boys don't talk to her till after her shower." She got into the front seat of the Bronco and backed up.

Sticking her head out the window, she called,

"I'm Sybil." Then this obviously close friend of Jan's tossed her hand out the window by way of farewell and drove off.

Speculation ran rampant in Kevin's mind. The "boys"?

Chapter Three

◆ ◆ ◆

ON HER FEET at last, Jan lurched for the doorway of her room. Grabbing for the doorjamb, she caught it and held firm. Then she leaned heavily against the wall for support as she croaked out a groggy, "Sybil?"

The movements she had heard earlier in the main room of the cabin had ceased, and now all was quiet. Making her way none too steadily to the kitchen in one corner of the large living area of the cabin, she squinted her eyes.

"Aw, Sybil, you old dear," she mumbled as she spied the pot of fresh coffee waiting for her. She poured a cup and perched herself on a tall stool beside a large butcher-block work table that dominated that corner.

Hunched over the cup held possessively in one hand, she supported her head on the palm of the other hand to keep it from falling off her shoulders.

A slight movement across the room caught her eye, and she shifted her head slightly. The spectral image of Kevin Toliver appeared before her not twenty feet away. Standing near the great stone fireplace that covered the entire rear wall of the cabin, he struck a relaxed pose, resting one arm on the mantel.

A dreamy expression came to Jan's face as she wallowed in her dream. He was so beautiful. Tall and powerfully built, with great wide shoulders that were now encased in a dark brown leather jacket zipped halfway up the front. The pale blue shirt underneath flattered his eyes. Open at the throat, the shirt revealed part of the mat of dark curly hair that covered his chest. Jan thought it looked particularly soft and inviting.

His lean hips and long muscular legs were encased in a pair of form-fitting jeans that enhanced the powerful appearance of his masculine form. Jan expelled a soft sigh of longing as the mirage shifted its weight from one leg to the other.

Jan was not surprised to see the image of Kevin Toliver standing in her living room. He had occupied most of her conscious and unconscious thoughts since she'd first encountered him the day before in the doorway of the boardroom. A familiar feeling of disappointment washed over her as she recalled the slim possibilities of ever seeing him again. She gave her

head a slight shake and moaned heavily in resigned hopelessness.

Kevin's heart rate had increased noticeably as
it beat painfully against the walls of his chest.
He had barely moved, but he felt as if he'd just
finished a marathon. His breath was labored, his
heart raced, and adrenaline shot through his
veins. If she didn't stop looking at him like that,
he was going to give in to his impulse to grab her
up, kiss the stuffing out of her, and carry her
back to her bed.

Dressed in a pair of tailored satin pajamas the
color of jade, she sat watching him, taking in
every nuance of his body. At one point her eyes
came to rest on his now-throbbing source of
maleness; Kevin thought he might pass out.

Her outfit did very little to conceal the firm,
round orbs of her breasts or the soft curves of
her hips. With incredulous eyes he watched as
her breasts formed peaks beneath the thin, silky
material covering them. His heart stopped and
his eyes shot to her face. None of what was happening to her body registered in her face. In a
state of numbed adoration, she merely continued to sit and peruse him with her eyes.

Recalling Sybil's warning, he didn't speak to
her. In fact, at this point he wasn't sure what to
say to her. He continued to stand quietly, making valiant efforts to maintain his control.

At last she released one final sigh and gave her
head a little shake. Rising from the stool with
her coffee cup in hand, she ambled off toward
the bathroom. As she passed by Kevin, he heard

her mumble something about "the powers of the mind" and "most incredible dreams."

As he listened to her taking her shower, Kevin continued his investigation of the cabin.

Standing at the rear of the house, he turned to face the front door. The structure was basically a large rectangle. To his left were two doors, one he knew led to Jan's bedroom, the other he assumed led to another. In front of him, to the left of the front door, was a large round oak dining table with five captain's chairs surrounding it. To the right of the door was the kitchen, its focal point the large worktable where Jan had been sitting. She had gone through a door off the kitchen, to Kevin's right, which was obviously the bathroom. Before him on a large oval woven rug sat two leather chairs on either side of an overstuffed sofa. Behind him was a solid wall of rock, which housed a huge fireplace with a rock mantel above and a hearth below.

Overall, it had a pleasing appearance of old-fashioned comfort and warmth mixed with modern technology. The appliances in the kitchen were contemporary. There was a television and an elaborate stereo system. In the loft above the living room Kevin had seen a skylight and a small home computer. Jan's office, he speculated. Everything had a clean shine to it. This remote cabin was obviously well loved and cared for.

"I thought maybe I had only dreamed you up," Jan said in her low, husky voice. Poised in the doorway of the bathroom, she wore a white terry-cloth bathrobe, her head turbaned in a towel. Hesitant, she started across the room toward her bedroom. "You're still here, so I guess it wasn't my imagination after all," she said.

When he made no reply, she stopped at the door of her bedroom and turned to face him again. "You know, someday I'd like to meet you on equal ground. I'm beginning to feel at a distinct disadvantage." She turned away with a wry smile.

"I sent a telegram," Kevin tried to explain again, almost apologetically.

"Living up here is an adventure in the reliability of modern technology. When something works the way it's supposed to, you don't take it for granted," she told him understandingly.

Chuckling, Kevin turned toward the mantel, as she left to get dressed. There were several pictures in ornate metallic frames, discolored with time, placed carefully on each end. On one end were three pictures, one of an older man with white hair and a much younger version of Sybil sitting on the steps of one of the cabins. The second was of a young dark-haired couple, each holding a small child in their arms. The third was an older picture of a young dark-haired man and a woman in a standard studio pose. The man in the picture looked vaguely familiar to Kevin, even though the woman had Jan's eyes and mouth.

On the other end of the mantel in wooden frames were pictures of two young boys. Their happy grins and sparkling green eyes resembled

Jan's, but their hair was a darker brown and lacked the reddish highlights of Jan's. Kevin guessed their ages at about three and five.

"They're a little on the short side, but they're definitely worth hurrying home to," Jan spoke from just behind Kevin.

He turned to see her amused smirk. His brow rose quizzically as he titled his head toward the pictures and said, "Your men?" A slow grin spread across his face.

Jan nodded. "Handsome devils, don't you think?" she teased.

Kevin's brows snapped down into a frown. "I thought you were single."

Her grin widening, she stated, "I am."

"Oh. You're divorced, then?"

"Nope. I was married once, though. For two and a half whole weeks. It was annulled two years ago."

"Then how . . . where . . ." He faltered, his mind spinning. The children certainly resembled her. Unwed mothers were not unheard of, but . . .

Jan began to laugh. It was a lovely sound, clear and uninhibited. "I inherited them," she said simply, then went on to explain. "They're my sister's children. This is her and her husband when the boys were younger. She and Donald died in an auto accident two years ago. I got custody."

"I see." He nodded his understanding slowly. "It must have been hard on you. Losing your sister and becoming the instant mother of two small children."

"Mmm. It was," she answered absently, as if recalling the memories. "Then I quit my job and we all moved out here from New York. A period of adjustment is a gross understatement for what went on here that summer." She smiled and shrugged as if to say it was a thing of the past and best forgotten.

"That's when you decided to become a planning consultant," he said, leading her to a subject that was common to both of them.

"Yes," she said, then added, "Would you like some coffee or something?"

"Coffee would be nice, thanks," he replied. As she turned from him, light from the setting sun beyond the open front door caught in her hair and reflected the auburn highlights. Her hair looked thick and soft, and he had a sudden urge to run his fingers through it over and over. It was still a little damp from her shower and seemed to have a life of its own. It curled and waved its way to her shoulders at its own discretion. Jan looked natural and at home here too—more relaxed now that she was on her own turf.

She had a clean, fresh country look about her as well as the sophisticated air he'd seen yesterday. She was a complete study in contradictions. Businesswoman and homemaker; soft, touchable country girl with an aloof city air.

"As a matter of fact, the idea of becoming an independent consultant was Gil Anderson's. He's an old fishing buddy of my grandfather's. My grandfather built both these cabins. I spent every summer here with him from the time I could first walk until I finished college. Even when I worked in New York, I spent all my vacation time here.

She had continued to speak while she poured the coffee. Handing him the cup, she adjourned to one corner of the sofa with another. He sat in the leather chair next to her.

"Anyway," she went on to say, "I've known Gil and his family for years. He thought with my earlier job training and what referrals he could get me from Toliver, Inc., and his other real estate contacts, that I could work out a nice little independent operation. Then, of course, you took me on permanently, and it's worked out great. I'm never away from home for more than a day or two at a time, and I've gone three or four months usually between trips.

"I do most of my land research here at home on my computer"—she motioned upward to the loft with her hand—"and Gil gives me computer time at the office for the bigger projects I do for your company," she finished almost breathlessly. It hadn't occurred to her until halfway through her dissertation to wonder just exactly why Kevin Toliver was sitting in *her* living room. She had been so unexpectedly pleased to see him that she'd just been soaking up his presence without a thought to his purpose for being there. An uneasy feeling told her that since they hardly knew each other, and the impression she'd been making on him for two days couldn't

be favorable, the reason wasn't personal. Therefore, it had to be business.

"So you prefer being an independent consultant as opposed to working for a firm?" she
heard him ask through her turmoil of thoughts.

"Yes, I . . ." She broke off her response as the
phone began to ring. It was a brief call, and
when she turned back to Kevin she was smiling
humorously. "You're arriving in Denver this
morning and would like to see me," Jan informed Kevin matter-of-factly, her eyes twinkling merrily. "They're getting better. You beat
your telegram by only eight hours this time. I
think the past record was forty-eight."

Her head turned sharply then toward the door
as she heard a car pull up outside the cabin.

Chapter Four

◆ ◆ ◆

THREE CAR DOORS slammed just seconds before
bedlam broke out in the cabin.

"Aunt Jan!"

"Aunt Jan!" heralded the arrival of the two little boys.

It was accompanied by a chorus of barking,
and Sybil chimed in with terse reminders to

"leave the dogs outside" and "wipe your feet, you two."

Jan had moved around to the back of the couch to face the whirling dervish entering the room. It was all hairy legs and tennis shoes; it had wagging tails and flailing arms. Kevin felt as though he ought to throw his body in front of Jan to protect her from attack, but she was laughing happily, her arms outstretched to embrace it.

A torpedo broke loose from the main body. It was a small boy with curly brown hair that probably wouldn't recognize a comb. His large green eyes, so like Jan's, took up much of his face. His sturdy little legs propelled him toward her. She went down on one knee to catch him, and when the two came together, the impact forced them to the floor, laughing, tickling, and giggling with glee.

Next came two dogs. An older black cocker spaniel lumbered up to Jan and sniffed the leg of her pants. Slowly he walked around the brawl on the floor and settled himself before the fireplace at Kevin's feet.

The second dog was much larger and of unknown pedigree. He had a huge head and a shaggy coat of long golden hair. His tastes were not as cultured as the spaniel's, and he stood above the pair on the floor, licking and nuzzling enthusiastically.

While Sybil remained at the door, watching the melee on the floor indulgently, the last of the pack, another young boy, taller, older and thinner than the first, made his way toward Jan. He had a pleased expression on his face and was grinning at the show. His pace was slower, however, as he wore a metal brace on his left leg that was attached to a special hard leather shoe with a thick leather sole. On the other foot he wore a black and white high-topped sneaker. The contrast sickened Kevin with sympathy.

This boy noticed Kevin sitting in the large leather chair and cast a friendly if timid smile toward him. Kevin smiled back and winked as if agreeing with the boy that the three on the floor were indeed a grand sight. Kevin noticed this boy's eyes were also similar to Jan's, with just a slight difference in the shape. His hair was darker and straighter than his brother's. Although he appeared warm and friendly, he had a decided solemnity to his personality that made him seem very vulnerable.

"Hi, Jeff," gasped Jan between giggles. Her hand shot out and grabbed his thin arm, and with a swift tug she jerked the boy down on top of dog and his brother and began to tickle him too. Soon he was flopping his arms about, laughing and gasping for breath just like the others.

The ruckus gradually relaxed and Jan sat like an Indian on the floor with the smaller boy on her lap and the other stretched out on the floor beside her.

Suddenly the younger boy took on an angry look and turned to his aunt. In a high, clear voice he blurted out, "Aunt Jan, Mrs. Silverman called Gramma's house this morning while we

were eating breakfast and she said that Baby
had run all the way over to her house in the
middle of the dark night and dug up all her buga
root. . . ."

"She said he dug up her begonia bulbs," the
older boy clarified passively.

". . . And she said if she ever saw him again,
she'd shoot a buck—"

"She said she'd shoot him with buckshot," the
older interjected while his brother continued,
barely pausing for air.

". . . And today at the Spencers' house, Nancy
told her mom that we don't take baths in the
house and that my whole family goes skinny-
dipping in our dirty old pond," Tommy informed his aunt indignantly.

"What did you tell her?" Jan asked, an anxious
note in her voice.

"I told her our pond wasn't dirty," he ended
with a shrug of simplicity.

Silence fell on the room. Jan heard a snicker
and glanced over at Kevin to see him red-faced
and near apoplexy from holding his laughter inside. Their eyes met and the two adults burst
into hearty laughter together.

After several minutes Kevin wiped a tear from
his eye and as he caught hers again, he mouthed
"skinny-dipping?" at her with a lecherous look in
his eyes.

Jan sobered as she watched his facial expression begin to change. His eyes darkened with
longing, holding hers, searching hers, delving
into her soul for an answer to his need. Kevin

drew his eyes away but didn't dispel his hold on her. A warm flush spread through her body as his eyes moved over it as if she were naked. His eyes caressed her skin and sent her pulse soaring. His gaze told her that he ached to touch what he saw and he wanted to conquer what he ached for.

The intensity of his naked desire made Jan tremble, but not in fear. This was not the first time she had had lustful thoughts of pressing herself to his warm nakedness. She, too, had entertained notions of memorizing his strong body with her hands, of tasting his skin with her tongue and nibbing his lower lip with her teeth.

But lust was lust, and a relationship based on physical attraction alone wasn't Jan's way. She lowered her eyes away from his, hoping he hadn't seen her own desire written in them. She could feel him still watching her, beckoning her to turn back to him, but she refused. It was too soon.

Recalling herself, she got to her feet, helped the boys to theirs and turned them toward Kevin. "Gentlemen," she addressed them formally, "this is Mr. Toliver. He's from New York. Kevin, my nephews, Jeff"—she indicated the older—"and Tommy."

Kevin stood to his full six feet three inches, watching the boys' eyes widen and their heads tilt back to look up at him. With a friendly grin he extended a hand to each of them in turn, pumping their small arms as if they were his equal.

"Jeff. Tommy. I'm pleased to meet you. I hope you'll do me the pleasure of showing me that pond sometime while I'm here." A glance at Jan told her he was hoping she'd come along.

Tommy, who wouldn't recognize a stranger if he met one, announced, "My birthday is Saturday and we're having a picnic at the pond. You can come if you want to." He paused, then added, "You don't even have to bring me a present if you don't want to."

"I'd like that," Kevin responded with pleasure, "if it's okay with your aunt."

The three pairs of eyes turned to Jan expectantly.

"Of course it's okay. The more the merrier, right, Tommy?" she said, strangely breathless once again.

"You going to feed us pretty soon?" came a voice from the kitchen corner. The forgotten Sybil was leaning back against the counter by the sink, arms folded over her abundant bosom, taking everything in with an astute eye.

"Oh," Jan said, startled, "of course." Turning to Jeff, she asked pointedly, "How'd the game go?"

Jeff opened his mouth to speak, but it was Tommy who reported. "It was great! Jeff made two goals and Mr. Simonson took us all for double-nutty chocolate dippers at Smitty's after the game. He said we had to eat all our dinner, too, or he'd be in lots of trouble." Tommy then turned to Kevin. "Wanna come see my Mighty Boarbon action figures? I don't have Delapado yet. Aunt Jan can't find him anywhere. You can wind up his arms and he'll knock over buildings."

"Well, if it's no trouble, I would like to see them," Kevin answered, straight-faced.

"Oh, it's no trouble—they're all over the floor in my room," Tommy answered brightly, and ran off down the hall with Jeff following in his wake.

As Kevin headed after them, Jan caught up with him and placed a hand on his forearm to stop him. They both felt an odd prickling sensation on contact; it tingled up their arms and tensed their muscles.

As Jan's hand fell away, she spoke softly, hesitantly. "Kevin, I'd like to invite you to stay for dinner, but when Jeff wins a game . . ." She paused with uncertainty. "Well, we have his favorite meal to celebrate." When he made no reply, she went on. "We have hot dogs and pork and beans," she finished in a rush.

"And there's not enough for me," he finished, his eyes twinkling in amusement at her discomfort.

"No, there's plenty," she gushed, embarrassed. "I just didn't think . . ."

"I would be honored if you'd let me stay for dinner," he said softly, sincerely, almost as a caress.

She beamed at him, her pleasure at his acceptance evident as she turned toward the kitchen. He grasped her hand to stall her and moved up behind her. When he lowered his head to her

ear, his lips purposely grazed her neck and earlobe, sending tremors of delight through her
body. "Jan, I'm curious. When Jeff loses a game,
what do you have for dinner?"

She tilted her head back and their eyes locked,
their noses almost touching. They could feel
each other's breath on their lips.

"We have hot dogs and pork and beans to relieve the agony of defeat."

On an impulse he brushed her lips with his,
then studied her face intently. After several seconds he smiled, his eyes lighting in appreciation.
He gave her hand a gentle squeeze, then turned
toward the boys' room.

The meal was a surprisingly nostalgic pleasure for Kevin. He remembered casual family
meals like this from his childhood, with his own
parents and his sister.

Jan told the boys and Sybil about her trips to
Seattle and Portland, omitting, he noticed, the
fact that she had gone without sleep in order to
get home a half day earlier. She explained the
added trip to New York as an honor to her, as
Mr. Toliver had invited her there expressly to
compliment her work at a meeting of his executive committee. Her voice indicated her gratification, and the boys seemed pleased for her.
Kevin recalled her time in New York as somewhat more stimulating than that, but concluded
that maybe sleeping on his couch all day hadn't
been quite the erotic experience for her as
watching her had been for him.

The boys' recitation of their day was a combined effort, resulting in a disruptive collage of the soccer game, their school play, and an extremely interesting review of local gossip by Tommy, who had overheard Sybil and Pete Jamison, the gas station attendant, swapping said information when they had stopped for gasoline that afternoon. Sybil's contribution to the conversation consisted primarily of correcting and embellishing on the juicier pieces of local news.

For his part, Kevin asked questions of the boys. From his questions of Jeff, he ascertained that the boys' soccer team was part of the Special Olympics program for handicapped children. The boy spoke unselfconsciously of how he had learned to kick the ball in a special way to keep from losing his balance and falling. His all-time favorite soccer hero was, of course, Pele. Then he stated proudly that players had to be six years old to play because Coach Simonson said that anybody younger couldn't control the ball as well as the six-year-olds.

Jan added that Mr. Simonson was a high school gym teacher in Boulder, although he lived in Pleasant Valley, and that during the summer he volunteered to coach the Special Olympics kids. Apparently, every afternoon he'd picked the boys up down at the tree stump and had taken them to Boulder for soccer practice. With a twinkle in her eye she went on to explain that they'd known Mr. Simonson for a long time, and he knew what a good sport Tommy was and had asked the boy to be the team mascot. Tommy grinned proudly.

When the meal was over and the boys were sprawled on the floor in the middle of the room playing with miniature race cars on a swirling plastic race track and the women were clearing the table, Kevin was overwhelmed by a feeling of loneliness. He was amazed that he hadn't realized before how empty his own life was. He had often experienced a feeling of discontentment, but he had blamed it on work, or the woman he was seeing at the time, or just about anything but loneliness or his lack of anyone to truly care for.

His own parents had died years before, and his sister and her husband lived in New Jersey. Although they would visit each other occasionally, they weren't very close. Then there was always his network of friends and business acquaintances, only a few with which he had close personal relationships.

The women in his life had decreased in numbers over the years. There were still the occasional nights of lustful endeavors, but for the most part the women he'd been meeting lately failed to catch and hold his interest. He'd found less disappointment in his work and eventually it had taken over his life completely. Mulling it over, he was now oddly disgruntled that for such a long time he'd been so absorbed in his job that he had totally neglected his personal life.

He envied Jan her courage to break away

from corporate security and set out on her own. Her ability to love astounded him. She had unselfishly turned her own life upside down to make a home for two small boys. His respect for her work dimmed in the light of his regard for her as a selfless, loving woman.

He watched her move around the cabin, wiping and cleaning. His desire for her body was as strong as ever, but the appeal was taking on new emotions. He still wanted to take her in his arms, hold her close, and make them one, but the compulsion to protect her from the rest of the world was overpowering.

Strangest of all, these new feelings didn't frighten him; they felt natural, and he welcomed them.

He was vaguely aware that bath time for the boys had arrived and that there were protests and grumblings about not being able to bathe in the pond. Jan's comments on the subject were lost to him as the bathroom door closed. With a smug grin on his face because he suspected the reason for the forgone trip to the pond, he glanced around the room to find Sybil watching him.

The older woman didn't speak at first, merely sat on the stool by the worktable and observed him keenly. After several minutes of mental debate she asked bluntly, "How long are you going to be around here?"

"I'm leaving Sunday."

"Well . . ." Her lips pursed together momentarily while she considered her next words. "Just don't hurt her."

"I won't," he said softly.

The boys eventually went to bed, and Sybil said good night and retired to her own cabin. Jan and Kevin were alone again. Recalling that discretion was the better part of valor, and not wanting to rush Jan, Kevin decided to take his leave before he did something foolish.

Jan walked him to the door and, noting only her own vehicles outside, inquired about his. He explained about the rental car, indicating he planned to trade it in for something more appropriate before Saturday, and she offered to walk down the road with him. Kevin protested, claiming it was too far for her to walk back alone in the dark. She laughed at him and proceeded out the door.

"It seems like a long way because it's all uphill, but it's really only about ten New York blocks to the tree stump from here. As for walking it in the dark, I'm very familiar with it. When I was a teenager, my dates would sometimes have the same problem with their cars that you did. I got used to it."

"So you walked this road a lot, huh?" he said, commenting inanely on what he was sure had been an active social life.

"Mmm," she confirmed without being specific.

"You know most everyone around here, then," he commented, thinking he could lead her into telling more about herself, particularly whether or not she was seeing anyone special.

Before he'd found out about "her men," the thought of her with another man had driven him nearly crazy. He still wanted her to come back and work in New York with him, but he finally admitted to himself that he could have offered her that through the mail. He had come himself purely to see her again.

"Yes," she was saying, "although I only came in the summer. My grandfather lived up here for years, so anyone who knew him eventually met us."

"Us?"

"My sister and me. Originally, he was from Boulder. He was an attorney. The first cabin—mine—was built as a summer retreat. As he got older, I think he had visions of a Walton's Mountain, though. He had only the one child, my mother, yet when I was born he started the second cabin. Four years later my mother died just two weeks after she gave birth to my sister . . . there were complications with the delivery. Anyway, my father came back only once after my mother's death, so my grandfather stopped with the second cabin. He planned to leave one to me and one to my sister."

"Why didn't your father come back in the summers with you and your sister?" Kevin asked. The night was quiet except for the steady sound of insects in the woods and an occasional bird trilling softly. Their footsteps crunched loudly but companionably along the road.

"He always told us he was too busy to come," she said, and Kevin sensed rather than heard a reluctance in her to discuss her father, almost as if talking about him were painful to her. "My grandfather used to say there were sleeping demons up here that Caroline and I would never see, but that they would always wake up and chase my father when he came here. That story was very cryptic when we were young, and it always made us feel sorry for our father. Now I suppose it isn't quite so mysterious—the demons were probably memories of my mother."

The sadness in her voice deepened at the hurtful memories. Kevin let his hand find and hold hers in a reassuring grasp. Silence surrounded them and drew them closer, making them acutely aware of each other and how totally alone they were, yet both felt comfortable and at ease, as if the other's mere presence was all each wanted.

When Jan finally broke the spell between them with words, Kevin was startled.

"Why did you come here, Kevin?" she asked softly in her low, raspy voice.

Never one to beat around the bush when a direct approach could convey so much more, he said, "Aside from wanting to see you again and feeling frustrated with the idea that you were so far away, I came to offer you the position of vice-president of operations at Toliver, Inc."

"But I . . ." She started to speak, but his fingers sought and found her lips to still them.

"Don't refuse me yet. I had no idea what I was

competing with here. I still want you. I just need time to consider a new plan of assault." He chuckled sensuously deep in his throat as the tips of his fingers outlined the shape of her lips. He brushed her bottom lip, taking in its softness and pliability before he said, "If you thought you heard a double entendre, you're right."

Slowly, he lowered his head. Pulling her lower lip down gently with his thumb, he touched it with his mouth and sucked gently once, then twice. He raised up then to run the tip of his tongue over her lips as his fingers had. Slipping his tongue between her lips, he teased the sensitive inner flesh.

She moaned softly and he brought his hands up to cup her face. As her body moved ever closer to his, he nipped at the corners and along the edge of her lower lip with his teeth.

Jan was close enough now for him to feel the rapid rise and fall of her breasts against his chest. Her body hung heavily from her neck as he supported her head. When at last she opened her mouth, he released a throaty growl of pleasure at her surrender and grabbed her up close to him. Placing his open mouth over hers, he savored his plunder.

She was warm and sweet like fresh sugar candy. Her tongue, shy at first, became bolder and teased his, touching, then darting away only to return and caress his slowly.

His hands, spread across her back, moved up and down several times, enjoying the feel of her closeness. They descended to cup her bottom gently before roaming up her soft hips to span her waist briefly. His large palms came to rest on the sides of her breasts and under her arms, where he pulled gently, stretching the already taut skin even tighter. He felt her knees give way as her passion overtook her, and he shifted his embrace, placing one hand at the nape of her neck and the other at the small of her back for support. He drew her close against the hard evidence of his own desire. When she groaned, he thought he would explode.

· The kiss went beyond satisfaction to create a need in Kevin to consume all of her. With an excruciating effort he pulled his lips away, then returned for one last tender touch.

He couldn't see her face, but he was extremely gratified by the way her body had and was still responding. He placed his right hand on her cheek and his voice broke as he spoke. "I came all the way from New York for that kiss," he said, "and I'll be back for more."

Chapter Five

◆ ◆ ◆

SEATED AT A computer terminal the next morning in an office reserved for her use at Toliver, Inc., in Denver, Jan's mind drifted. Absently, she began to whistle blissfully. She marveled at the kiss she and Kevin had shared the night before. Her heart felt light and her mind tittered at the thought that she would see him again the following day at Tommy's birthday party. In fact, her whole body quaked at the thought.

Over and over she contemplated a relationship with Kevin. It was definitely enticing. Never before had she been so deeply moved by anyone. No effort was required for her to bring back the feeling of his arms around her or for her to recall the exquisite torture of his lips. Even at her memories her blood began to bubble with an effervescent excitement.

But how were she and Kevin going to have any kind of decent relationship when he lived in New York and she lived in Pleasant Valley, Colorado?

"Oh, drat!" She spoke out loud as much to her

muse as to the terminal in front of her. "Save data?" had flashed across the bottom of her screen and with no thought in her head but one of Kevin, Jan had pressed N for no.

"Dope! Now you've done it," she wailed disparagingly to herself, having inadvertently erased all her statistics on both Seattle and Portland that had taken the last hour and a half to feed into the computer. Jan folded her arms across the top of the terminal and dropped her head on them in despair. If she hadn't been so wrapped up in Kevin, this wouldn't have happened. Now she'd have another hour and a half of very boring work to repeat.

"Having trouble?" came a resonant voice from the doorway.

Startled, Jan jerked and swiveled in her chair to face him. The frenzy at seeing Kevin again was acknowledged in the back of Jan's mind and deep in her heart, but it was pushed aside as a flood of culpability and disparity engulfed her.

"Oh, Lord, you scared me," she said for lack of anything else to say.

"Sorry," he said in a genial tone as he approached her. Perching himself on the corner of her desk, he grinned, merriment dancing in his eyes. "I know a little about computers. Can I help?"

In exasperation she turned on him. "Yes! You can wear a bell around your neck," she spat out. "Every time we meet, I find myself in a most awkward position. It's very irritating. I'm beginning to feel like the village idiot."

Kevin had been regarding her from the doorway. Today she was somebody else yet again. She was dressed in a cheery yellow linen business suit and a soft white blouse with a lazy bow at the neck. Her hair was swept up into a rich auburn twist on top of her head. The only deviance in her role as the liberated female executive was that she had been whistling while she worked. Kevin didn't think he'd ever seen a businesswoman whistle before. And it didn't seem like the chic, refined thing to do in front of a computer. But that Jan would whistle exhilarated him. Tenderness warmed his heart as he watched her pout and feel foolish for being the most unique, intriguing woman he'd ever met.

"Just once I'd like to be doing something impressive or at least something normal when you see me," she went on dejectedly.

Reaching over, he curled his finger under her chin and raised her face to his. "I am impressed, Jan. Very impressed," he said soothingly. "You're intelligent, warm, loving, and beautiful. I am very impressed."

She rewarded him with a weak smile. "I never sleep through board meetings or stare rudely at people for hours without speaking to them, and I hardly ever erase hours of work on a computer. It's just not me."

"You do like to beat a dead horse, though, don't you? Wednesday and Thursday you were asleep on your feet and you have nothing to feel bad about there, and even I've been known to screw up a computer program now and again," he said, dismissing her anxiety. "How about we start over. I'll promise that if I ever come into a room and find you doing something strange, I'll leave immediately, okay?" he teased.

Giving over to his goodwill, she smiled her gratitude. "Okay."

With a back-to-business attitude, he asked, "How much longer will you be at this? I want to ask you out to lunch."

Groaning, she said, "I'll be another couple of hours now, I'm afraid. Will that be too late for you?"

He grinned. "Not at all. I have a meeting with your friend Gil Anderson in half an hour. I was going to ask you to wait for me."

Such a nice grin, she thought to herself. Jan's anticipation dulled the dread of retyping her research.

Gil Anderson was out of his office when Kevin arrived a few minutes early for their appointment. Sitting in a chair in Gil's office, Kevin mulled over his problem with getting Jan to accept the position in New York. Why should she want to leave Colorado? Her family, home, and work were here. Reluctantly, he admitted that he couldn't see her living in the city again. She belonged here in the sunshine and open air. She was clean and fresh and wholesome; she was part of that mountain she lived on.

For selfish reasons he wanted her in New York not only for the company, but for his own sake. The more he saw of her, the more he wanted to see her. Time between their encounters dragged on endlessly for him. He felt physical pain at the thought of leaving her behind come Sunday. He had to think of some way to drag her off that mountain.

"Kevin," boomed a voice behind him. "Good to see you again. You don't get out here as often as you used to, and we hardly had time to say hello yesterday," the man accused Kevin as he came around to shake his hand vigorously.

"Gil, how are you?" Kevin returned.

"Good," he said flatly. "Tell me, did you find Jan's place yesterday? Those places out in the dinglebushes are impossible to find unless you know exactly which two trees to drive between," the man said, chuckling good-humoredly. Gil was a big man, as wide as a door and only an inch or two shorter than Kevin. He'd always reminded Kevin of a Viking, with his blond hair, blue eyes, and loud, reverberating voice. A jovial man in his late fifties, Gil had always been diligent in his work on behalf of Toliver.

Relating the drive out to the cabin and the need to get a different rental vehicle, Kevin then launched into his impressions of the terrain. Telling Gil how impressed he had been with the beauty of the land clarified in his mind the fact that he truly did enjoy Colorado's wide, open spaces, its wilderness and its majesty. Again he felt a pang of guilt for wanting to have Jan in New York. How could he ask her to leave?

"Did you get a chance to meet the boys?"

"Oh, yes." Kevin's face took on an expression

of humor and affection. "They're a pair, aren't they?" Grinning, he shook his head thoughtfully. "Tommy invited me to his birthday party at the pond tomorrow." His hand over his heart indicated his proper humility at the honor.

Gil leaned back in his chair on the other side of his desk and rubbed his chin with his hand. "That pond. Have you seen it yet?" Kevin indicated that he hadn't. "Originally it was just a stream that passed through a clearing in the back acreage of that plateau. One year the old man decided that what he wanted, instead of just that little stream, was a pond to swim in back there. He conned me into chopping down this huge tree that grew beside the stream . . . he had heart problems, you know . . . anyway, we got the damned tree cut down and then the old man took a few sticks of dynamite out there and stuffed them under the stump. I'll never forget it." He shook his head, laughing softly to himself. "He blew up the stump and not only did he get himself a crater for his pond, he damn near brought the rest of the mountain down on top of himself."

"That's getting a swimming hole the hard way," Kevin uttered.

"No, no . . ." Anderson put his hands up to show he wasn't finished. "What he got was a bog!" He laughed heartily now. "The hole filled to the top with mud. The old fella was fit to be tied. He finally had to pay a landscaper and an excavator to go up there and make him a decent swimming pool. I don't think Sybil ever let him live that down."

"Sybil was his wife then . . . but not Jan's grandmother?"

"That's right. She's Tom's second wife. She was thirty or so when he married her, and he was sixty. Said she gave him a new lease on life . . . and I guess that's a fact. They were married almost twenty-two years before he died last year."

"I didn't realize it had been so recent."

Gil was nodding. "It was a bad time for Jan . . . Sybil too. Tore 'em up." Speculatively, he continued. "Maybe if he'd been sick awhile it might have helped them accept it. He wouldn't admit his true age, and it didn't show. He'd been swimming in that damned cold water and a few minutes after he got out he just keeled over."

"Jan and the boys were out there with him. She worked CPR on him for nearly an hour before the boys and Sybil got the volunteer rescue squad up there from Pleasant Valley to help her. He never did regain consciousness and died during the night at the hospital in Boulder, but Jan sure fought like hell to keep him here," he finished in admiration and sympathy for the girl.

Kevin was silent, reflecting on his ever-changing picture of Jan Harper.

"Things are sort of leaning toward the Portland site right now, the economic situation being what it is with both Grayson's and the Electrotech factory going under. There'll be a large semi-skilled labor force for you to tap. The land is good for the price, although it could be a little more centrally located. That way . . ." She trailed off, realizing Kevin wasn't listening. She watched him as he idly played with the spoon beside his coffee cup, flipping it over and over with his long fingers. His hands were big, with long, tapering fingers. They looked powerful, but she already knew they could be tender and gentle as well.

The restaurant they had agreed on was quiet now, as it was between the lunch and dinner hour. Several other tables were occupied by women sipping coffee after what looked like a shopping spree from all the boxes and bags at their feet. Men were talking business with papers spread out on tops of the tables. To their left was a couple who were obviously in love, their hands touching as they passed secretive glances to each other.

Jan turned back to her table and found Kevin watching her. He had apparently noticed that she had stopped speaking because of his lack of attention.

There was a sheepish half smile on his face, and his eyes were apologetic.

"I'm sorry," he murmured. "What were you saying?"

She grinned, feeling as if she had a slight upper hand with him for a change. "You'll just have to read my report when it comes out," she teased.

"Will you deliver it in person?"

"Sure. With my very own hands I'll take it to the post office and deliver it into the mail."

"That's as far east as you'll go with it?"

A wary look crossed over her face. Kevin wouldn't understand the pain a move back to New York would cause her. The life she left behind was riddled with conflict and misery. She had cut all ties to that city to come to the only place in her life she had ever known contentment and peace. She wanted to explain it to him; she wanted him to understand.

"Kevin," she started.

"Jan, I know what I'm asking is too much. You have a good life here, and I can't blame you for not wanting to leave it." He paused, covering her hand with his, brushing the knuckles gently with his thumb. A tingly heat stole up her arm as he went on. "It's just that I can't . . . I . . ." he faltered, unwilling to admit his selfishness to her. "I'd very much like to have you on my staff. Nevertheless, I accept your decision." His reluctance was obvious in both his expression and his voice. "But please don't hold it against me if I'm a sore loser. I haven't had much experience at it, thank God."

"Kevin, I am sorry," she said sincerely.

"Can I at least have a consolation prize?" he asked in feigned dejection.

"Sure. What?"

"Stay in Denver this afternoon. Show me the sights. I haven't been here in a few years. Have dinner with me tonight," he demanded hopefully.

"Ah, Kevin," she said, dismayed, "I can't. I've been gone all week and I have a ton of—" She stopped and gave him a wily, suggestive grin as she went on. "Instead of Denver, how would you like an in-depth tour of Pleasant Valley? I'll give you a tour while I run my errands and do a few chores. I'll even treat you to dinner at Smitty's with the boys after soccer practice," she said as if that were the cherry on top.

Kevin didn't care where he had to go, he just wanted to be with her. On the way back to the office to pick up her Jeep, she informed him she'd have to go inside briefly to change her clothes.

He was waiting outside, prepared to follow her up the mountain when she returned. She was wearing a tailored forest-green shirt made of a silky material. It had long sleeves that she'd rolled up to her elbows and was buttoned down the front. The tails were tied in a knot under her breasts. Hip-hugging, thigh-clinging jeans made her legs look long and willowy. Her waist was cinched by a thin leather belt with a small silver clasp. She looked extremely sexy and provocative, and his pulse ran wild. As she walked to her car with a confident strut, Kevin watched her knowingly.

She was purposely making his trip back to New York as difficult for him as possible, and the idea pleased him, filling him with inspired thoughts of his own.

On the winding country roads to Pleasant Valley, Kevin was oblivious to the splendid scenery. He could barely keep himself on the road. All he could see was Jan as she sped along the highway.

The wind tore her hair from its topknot and was blowing the russet strands wildly about her face. In the bright red Renegade she took on a carefree, untamed appearance that stirred up some wild and primitive responses in Kevin as well.

An in-depth tour of Pleasant Valley is what she had offered, and that's exactly what he got. A small community, it had one main street, and Jan took Kevin into almost every establishment.

She filled her gas tank at the station on the outskirts of town. Now driving a four-wheel-drive pickup truck, Kevin decided to fill his as well, to ensure the trip back to Denver. While he used the full-service island, she the self-service, they were regaled for some time by the famous Pete Jamison, the local off-the-air newscaster.

They drove into town and parked in the Laundromat parking lot. From there they walked down the street, stopping at the post office to pick up her mail, the drugstore for a prescription for Jeff, and a dress store at which Jan had previously bought a dress and left it for some alterations. Taking the dress and slinging it over his shoulder in the most natural way, Kevin placed a possessive arm lightly around her shoulders and they continued on to a small grocery store. They spent a very domestic hour there comparing tastes in food and laughing together as Kevin pestered her to buy cheap wine instead of milk, his rationale being that it would make them mellow and put the boys completely out of commission. His wickedly suggestive eyes relayed his motives.

Jan hadn't had so much fun in ages. They laughed and giggled like children. They discovered common interests and tastes. Both enjoyed reading, he science fiction, she romantic novels. He teased her about "swirling, curving, soaring, driving, exploding" emotionalism and she kicked back with "short-circuiting invaders and mutant plants," saying it wasn't surprising that he'd found Tommy's Boarbon action figures fascinating. Sheepishly, he confessed his favorite was Telescopo who, when his ear was turned, extended a third eye out of the top of his head.

Kevin was a delightful companion, friendly, witty, and intelligent. She proudly introduced him to the shop owners and other patrons, all of whom were her friends. He shook hands and talked congenially with the men and flirted a little with the women. He seemed comfortable talking to the people of the town, and they responded to him in kind.

The sensations she experienced were varied but always pleasurable. There was always the thrill of his close presence. If she walked away from him while he finished a conversation, she knew his eyes followed her, possessive and watchful. It made her feel safe, protected, and wanted. And the ever-returning hand on her shoulders, on the bare small of her back, produced a prickling sensation that ran up and down her spine and settled in a knot low in her abdomen. The more he touched her, the more of her body she wanted touched.

Overwhelming her was the added attraction of his physical magnificence. Tall and built large, he made her feel exquisitely feminine. Her body responded to his overt and covert glances. Several times she'd caught his sharp blue eyes focused on the knot she'd tied between her breasts, as if considering the possibilities of its somehow coming loose. His eyes were wonderful. They laughed and teased, sobered and watched, caressed and desired. She liked watching his mouth too. It was sensuous and pliant. The lean lines of his face were strong and expressive. He was all hard muscle. There was obvious strength in his broad shoulders and chest, and power in his firm thighs. His trim hips and flat abdomen bespoke a potent energy of their own.

Having left his leather jacket in the truck, he wore his off-white dress shirt open at the neck and his sleeves rolled up to mid-forearm. The hair on his chest revealed at the V of his shirt was black and curly and very inviting. His form-fitting jeans were worn and looked comfortable.

As her eyes retraced their trail back up his masculine form, Jan saw that he had finished putting the sacks of groceries in the back of the Jeep and was watching her watch him.

"So, what do you think?" he asked, his expression staid. She knew her emotions were written all over her face and decided to be truthful.

"I think you are a very nice person, Kevin. I like you very much."

Gratified, he smiled at her. "Good. The feeling is mutual. What's next? Can we eat now? I'm starving."

"You sound like Tommy," she exclaimed, laughing. "And, no, we can't eat yet . . . but soon," she added as he started to complain like Tommy would. Walking to the opposite side of the Jeep, she threw back a canvas tarp to reveal three large stuffed duffel bags and as many cardboard boxes. "First we do laundry."

"Laundry? My dear Jan, do you know to whom you are speaking? I'm president and principal stockholder in a company I founded! I don't do windows, and I certainly don't do laundry!" he said, feigning indignance. "I'm a carefree bachelor, a dashing man-about-town. Have you got any idea what this will do to my reputation?"

All this was said as he followed her into the Laundromat. He watched as she dug several dollar bills from deep inside the front pocket of her jeans.

Jan gave the money to Kevin. "Go get some quarters, Mr. Big Shot. You're with me tonight, and I like slumming it." She grinned, showing off the delightful dimple in her cheek.

"On one condition," he stated. When she raised her brows in question, he motioned toward her pocket and murmured, "Next time you need money from there, please allow me to get it for you."

"Why, Mr. Toliver, you are so gallant."

"My dear Ms. Harper, it is but one of the many things I'd love to do for you." He swooped down and bussed her lips with his, then moved on to change the dollar bills.

Jan bent over and began sorting the clothes. With his hands full of quarters Kevin returned to an enticing display of her lovely posterior as she leaned over her task.

"Lord. Doing laundry just keeps getting better and better. How come no one ever told me what could be seen in a Laundromat?" he asked, his brow wrinkled as if truly bewildered.

Slowly she rose and turned toward him. She glanced around the room, seeing what she hadn't thought to notice before; they were now alone—completely and totally alone.

"Are you trying to embarrass me?" she asked softly, her skin already warming as she watched his eyes darken and intensify their scrutiny.

"Yes," he said in a stage whisper, "I enjoy knowing I'm getting to you. And I love the way you blush."

"Two can play that game, Kevin," she gloated.

"Games for two are the kind I delight in," he said. He reached out and took her by the hips. Pulling her toward him as he leaned back against the counter behind him, he positioned her between his legs. "Speaking of delights . . . have I told you yet that I think you're one?"

"One what?" she said absently as she refrained

from touching the dark hair that curled softly near the top of his ear.

"I think you are a delight."

"You do?" Unable to resist, she fingered the curl.

With a light touch on her chin he brought her face back to his. They studied each other's eyes, both coming to the same conclusion.

"Kiss me, Jan," he ordered her in a low, husky voice.

Sending sidelong glances in either direction, she smiled shyly. "Now? What if someone comes in?"

"What if they do? The whole town has diagnosed me as lovesick. They won't be surprised to find us kissing."

"They won't?" she uttered numbly as she felt herself being drawn deeper and deeper into the blueness of his eyes, the strength of his embrace, the warmth of his body.

"No. In fact they'll think you're as wonderful as I do for taking mercy on me." Then, all joking aside, he whispered, "Kiss me." He pulled her closer and the zippers on their jeans pressed tightly together.

She leaned close to his face, her lips grazing but not completely touching his. "Do you mean" —she tickled his lips with hers, half-afraid to let loose of the lighter mood as Kevin had—"that you want me to press my lips to yours. . . . Or would you prefer . . ."

He groaned and captured her mouth with his. Quickly his tongue slipped past her lips and teeth to taste and explore her with a burning kiss.

Forehead to forehead, eyes closed, they paused to cherish the moment, to savor their closeness.

"Jan. Jan," Kevin rasped in wonderment, while Jan sighed her contentment, her head still reeling.

"Aunt Jan! What are you doing?"

Cheek to cheek, they turned to find Tommy marching in with his hands on his hips and repugnance on his face. Jeff followed Tommy with Sybil taking up the rear. All three watched as Jan blushed and Kevin grinned merrily.

"Nice," he approved under his breath for only her to hear, describing both the kiss and her blush.

Meanwhile Tommy had continued. "Were you kissing Mr. Toliver?"

Rapidly going over a list of possible answers, she opted for honesty. "Yes, I was, Tommy."

"And you let her?" Tommy turned on Kevin. He had obviously thought Kevin a better man than this.

Releasing Jan as she pulled a short distance away, Kevin looked down at the boy indulgently. "When you get older, Tommy, you're going to find out that kissing ladies like your Aunt Jan is very, very nice." His eyes roamed over her face, then turned back to Tommy. "Doesn't it make you feel good when she gives you kisses and hugs?"

"Yeah," he admitted. Kevin could almost see

the gears grinding in Tommy's head as he thought about it. Sensing a sticky situation coming on, Kevin bent down to lift the boy up onto his shoulders and headed for the door as the child began to speak.

"That's different, though, isn't it? When she kisses me it's cuz she loves me. Does it mean love when big people kiss? Do you love my aunt Jan? Jeff says kissing is yucky. . . ."

Through the window of the Laundromat Jan saw Kevin answer Tommy's questions but couldn't hear it. Trepidation stiffened her muscles at the sight of the big man talking to the little boy.

After filling the washers with her laundry and depositing the quarters, Jan added the detergent. Then she and Sybil joined the men in the parking lot.

The boys were entertaining Kevin with their repertoire of elephant and giraffe jokes and Kevin was laughing appreciatively. Jan's throat constricted as she watched the three of them together. It was hard for her to reconcile herself to the fact that Kevin wasn't staying and she wasn't following.

The usually quiet but always blunt-spoken Sybil remained silent but eyed Jan thoughtfully.

Smitty's was a multipurpose restaurant on the far end of the main trek. It served breakfast, lunch, and dinner at tables positioned in a semi-circle around a large dance floor with a short stage on one corner. The dance floor was also used for the Women's League fashion show in the fall and spring, and for local club meetings. It functioned as a dance floor only on Friday and Saturday nights. The soccer coach, Stan Simonson, was a member of a local country-western band, and they provided the music.

Saturdays and weekday afternoons Smitty's was also the local teenage hangout. And always, to the boys' delight, it was an ice cream parlor.

In the front of the building were booths separated from the dining room by smoky glass bricks. They sat in a booth now, with Tommy on a chair in the aisle. The boys were finishing up chocolate sundaes with extra nuts while the adults drank after-dinner coffee.

"Hot dogs one night, hamburgers the next. I hope we don't destroy your sophisticated palate," Jan teased Kevin, her eyes shining like emeralds, her body warm as her arm and hip and thigh rubbed against his.

"Don't you have hot dogs in New York? Jeff won't be too happy going there for his operation if you don't have hot dogs. That's his favorite thing," announced Tommy around a spoonful of ice cream.

"What operation? When are you coming to New York?" Kevin asked Jan, concerned for Jeff but also hopeful of seeing her again.

Smiling gently at Jeff, she answered simply, "Jeff needs an operation pretty soon that might fix his leg. There's a chance we may have to go to New York for it."

The subject was obviously a difficult one for

both Jan and Jeff. Kevin wanted to know more about it but decided to wait for a better time.

However, it was Sybil who changed the subject. "And then maybe you can get your life straightened out and change that stupid name you're using," she admonished, her disapproval evident.

Totally perplexed now, Kevin turned to Jan. "What stupid name changed?"

Jan grimaced and sighed in resignation.

"Harper was my husband's name. When I got my annulment, my father and I weren't getting along. . . ." She paused. "It's not something I'm proud of doing, but to punish him I refused to take his name back. It was also a bitter punishment for myself. I was hurt and feeling like a grade A jerk for marrying Tony Harper in the first place. I kept his name to remind myself what doing something stupid felt like."

"You were married to Tony Harper? Blond guy? An attorney?" Seeing her nod, he was incredulous. "I know him. *He's* the jerk, and a louse to boot. . . ." He stopped, realizing what he was saying about her judgment.

Dazed, he turned back to face the others before he said anything else to hurt her. Tony Harper was a fraudulent, money-grabbing social climber. Kevin's friend, Jeff Manning, whom he was now negotiating the sale of a subsidiary with, had some problems with Harper a few years back. Kevin couldn't remember the whole story, but Manning had had Harper fired from the firm of attorneys that handled most of Manning Industries' holdings. More recently there had been some ugly rumors of Harper's escapades with the eighteen-year-old daughter of yet another wealthy man. What could he possibly have wanted from Jan? She had been moving her way up the corporate ladder back then. Harper must have wanted to hang on to her shirttail and go up with her. The thought of Tony Harper's hands on Jan made Kevin physically ill.

It was with an angry scowl on his face that Kevin encountered the nefarious Mrs. Silverman. She was an older woman with a yellowish complexion and a pinched face. She had a sour-looking expression as she leaned over and whispered to a nondescript woman beside her, tossing a glance in Kevin's direction.

Sybil and the boys were preparing to leave, when the woman descended on them. Kevin could feel Jan stiffen beside him.

"Jan. Sybil. Boys," the woman greeted them in a too-sweet voice. Interesting combination, Kevin thought—sweet and sour.

"Is this your new young man, Jan?" she inquired, insinuating by her tone that if he was, she'd know all about it soon enough.

"This is my friend Kevin Toliver from New York, Mrs. Silverman," Jan introduced them politely, her tone cool.

"Seeing dear Jan out with a man again is indeed encouraging," she said to Kevin. "We were all beginning to despair that she would ever seek out male companionship again after her dreadful experiences, the poor dear." She paused only to take in more air. "Stanley will be ecstatic to see you going out again, Jan." Back to Kevin, she said, "And you, young man, had better beware. Stanley has been after Jan for years, and he's practically a father to these dear boys," she finished with a grimace at the boys.

Stanley? Now who the hell is Stanley? Kevin wondered malevolently.

"Ruth," came a harsh warning from Sybil while Jan seethed.

Ruth Silverman merely continued, undaunted. "That reminds me, Jan, you really must exert more control over that big dog of yours. He has completely ruined my begonia bed this year. Really, dear, I'd hate to have to call the authorities out on this problem. Good evening, all," she finished, and sailed out of the door.

"Who's that she's gonna call, Aunt Jan? Is that the police? Is that what she's gonna do? Call the police on Baby?" sputtered Tommy angrily.

"That's what she says, Tommy."

"That yellow-lipped lemon licker . . ." Tommy started.

"Tommy!" Jan bit her cheeks to keep from giggling. "Where did you hear that?"

"That's what Petey at the gas station says she is. He says she's an old spoon who just likes to keep things stirred up, and I don't like her." Tommy was furious.

Softly, but firmly, Jan reprimanded him.

"That's okay, Tommy, you don't have to like

her, but calling her names and saying bad things about her only makes you seem as nasty as she is. Basically you're doing what she does. See?" He nodded in understanding. "Sometimes what you think and feel about someone is better left unsaid. Most often it's best just to stay away from people like that. Then their nastiness won't rub off on you. Okay?" she finished.

"You won't let her take Baby to jail, will you?" he asked anxiously.

"No, I won't. And she won't shoot him, either, so don't worry."

"Okay." He seemed reassured; however, Kevin noticed that Jeff was being quieter than usual and looked a little culpable.

Chapter Six

◆ ◆ ◆

IT WAS NEARLY seven-thirty by the time Sybil and the boys drove back to the cabins and Kevin and Jan returned to the Laundromat to take the clean clothes out of the washers and put them in dryers.

They sat on collapsible metal chairs near a large table used for folding clothes. They were quiet, each consumed with thoughts of their own.

Unable to bear the silence any longer, Jan broke it with the first thing that came to mind. "My grandfather always said the reason he never bought a washing machine and dryer was that doing the laundry was the only excuse he could think of to come to town. He grew his own garden and Sybil canned most of it, so they didn't need much in the way of groceries. Her garden is just a small summer garden now. They didn't eat very much red meat, and my grandfather and Gil Anderson fished a lot and froze that," she prattled on. "He liked being up at the cabins but felt he shouldn't lose contact with the people. He said people thought he was strange enough without becoming an eccentric recluse as well."

A thick silence fell over the big room as Kevin remained quiet, not knowing what to say, wanting to know so much about her and feeling his time slipping away.

Jan went on nervously. "I think I'll add on another room to put a washer and dryer in. I come to town enough that I don't need to use the laundry as an excuse." If he didn't say something soon, she thought she would die. She should never have told him about Tony Harper. He could only think one thing. . . .

"Tell me about Jeff's leg," he said suddenly out of the blue.

"Jeff's leg?" It was the last thing on her mind at the moment.

"I assumed it was a congenital defect. One leg is shorter than the other, right?"

"Yes and no," she said, rubbing her hand over her brow, wondering where to begin. "Yes, one leg is shorter than the other, but just slightly at this point, and no, it's not congenital."

He was listening closely, his concern and curiosity obvious.

"Both Jeff and Tommy were in the car accident that killed my sister and her husband," she said, her voice calm and steady, her features thoughtful. "It happened in early January in upstate New York about two and a half years ago. The roads were icy and covered with snow. They ran into the back of a trailer truck." Her voice and expression became detached as she went on. "I saw pictures of the accident scene and later they showed me pictures of the damage to the car. The front was bashed in horribly, but the rear of the car just past the front doors was still almost perfectly intact. The roof was folded like an accordion toward the back—the tail of the truck stopped at the back of the front seat." She shook her head slightly. "It was as if only Caroline and Donald were meant to die, but not the boys.

"Thank God they were in safety seats. Tommy was only seventeen months old. He was unconscious for several hours with a concussion. Other than a few tiny cuts from the flying glass and some bruises, especially where the straps from the seat had caught him, he was fine and running down the hospital corridors after a few days."

Jan got up as the lights started going off on the four dryers she was using. After opening the door of one of the machines, she reached in and scooped up a load of clothes and brought them back to the table to fold. Taking his cue from her, Kevin did the same. They were alone in a room full of washers and dryers, the owner having gone home to dinner. The machines had all stopped. They stood side by side companionably, folding clothes.

"Jeff had cuts and bruises all over too. He was conscious the whole time but shocked and confused and in pain. He had also fractured his left femur, the long bone in his thigh." She paused for a moment, collecting her thoughts. "Here's where it gets complicated. I don't know how familiar you are with the way the body grows, but the poor doctor had to literally draw me pictures." She chuckled, remembering. "Anyway, the bones grow in the shaft—the long rodlike part of the bone—especially lower in the shaft near the joints. Jeff's fracture was low on the shaft, just above the knee. He went the whole route—traction, a cast clear up to his little rear end, then crutches. The doctor told me in the beginning that the fracture was in the area crucial for the growth of the bone, and if there was enough trauma to the tissue, there was a chance that Jeff's leg wouldn't grow. Well, it would grow, but at a slower rate because of the injury, and Jeff would have a leg one or two inches shorter than the other, maybe more. Only time would tell."

Glancing at Kevin, who was listening intently and folding jeans and cords, she smiled warmly. "Following so far?"

With a nod and a grin he replied, "Right behind ya, honey. When did you find out his left leg was shorter?"

"Last summer. Seven-sixteenths of an inch. We had pretty much accepted the fact that he would have to wear lifts in his shoes and maybe thick-soled shoes on one foot." She paused and shifted the position of her hips uncomfortably. With a pained expression on her face she looked at the empty wall and went on. "You know what he told me about his leg being shorter? He told me it was better than being dead." Her eyes clouded and she dropped her head.

Kevin's heart tore, the pain intense as he empathized with both Jan and Jeff. He put a hand on each of her shoulders and drew her to him.

Jan didn't cry, but she let Kevin hold her. She listened to the steady thumping of his heart and let the warmth of his embrace spread through her. Not once from the time the police had called her that night until now had anyone held her or offered such sincere compassion. Not at Caroline's funeral, not during the long hours at the hospital, not after the angry words she and her father had exchanged, not even the afternoon she had received her annulment papers. No one had held her or accepted her pain. Not until Kevin.

After three short days he was letting her hurt and was comforting her with his strong, healthy spirit. People she'd known all her life hadn't let her cry out her pain. Sybil and her grandfather hadn't allowed her any despair. They all knew she had to survive, that she would survive, and they had left her alone to find her own source of strength to go on.

Gratitude overcame her, and with unshed tears turning her eyes to shimmering pools of green seawater, she brought her head up from his chest and placed her right palm along the side of his head. She tried to memorize his face once again and finally, in a faltering whisper, she said, "You are a very kind man, Kevin Toliver." She stretched upward and laid the most tender of kisses on his lips, then returned her head to his chest.

Kevin was deeply moved. His arms tightened instinctively to protect her from more pain. He was stunned when he realized that he would and could, without hesitation, kill with his bare hands anyone who ever hurt her again. It was quite a blow to an even-tempered man who was slow to anger and even slower to strike. The primitive urge to protect his mate consumed his rational mind.

Several minutes passed before he gently asked, "So, why does Jeff wear the brace if elevated shoes would be enough?"

Pulling away with a weak smile, she went back to folding before she continued with Jeff's story.

"Last fall Jeff started saying his leg hurt. Progressively over a couple of weeks the complaints and discomfort increased to the point where I thought I ought to take him back to the doctor. What had happened, basically, is that while playing sometime, he had cracked the bone—they called it a hairline fracture. Anyway, he had this thin break in the bone at the site of his original fracture. It turns out, for several possible reasons—age, diet, enzymes, lack of minerals in the water . . . whatever—his bone wasn't as stong as it should be. It had healed straight, but it wasn't strong. This in itself is easily remedied too. We're going to get Jeff a bone graft from his hipbone to make the femur strong."

"They can do that anywhere, can't they? What was all that about New York?" Kevin asked.

Taking a long, deep breath, Jan patiently continued.

"I wanted to have the grafting done last winter when we first found the problem, but Jeff's orthopedic surgeon said there was a doctor in New York who was doing some experimenting with a growth enzyme called ACTH, bone grafts, and a special diet in cases like Jeff's. Ordinarily, Jeff's injury would be too old to work with. They like fresh breaks because they wouldn't want to rebreak a perfectly strong, mended leg. But since Jeff's fracture is only partially mended and weak at that, the doctor in Denver thought we should at least try and see if Dr. Canal in New York would consider Jeff.

"The brace is mostly for looks. It keeps Jeff

from playing and running too hard, or bumping his leg with enough force to do more damage. The padded shoe acts as a shock absorber to prevent him from jarring it too hard.

"I sent all his medical and surgical files to this Dr. Canal in April. He called once and had Dr. Pierce in Denver run some additional tests, but we're still waiting for word."

"What happens if nothing can be done in New York?"

"Then we go back to plan A. The original bone graft and elevator shoes." She grinned at him, her tone lighter.

"Are you really as easy about that as you sound?" He was watching her closely.

"Yep. Jeff's a good kid and I love him. There's not a thing wrong with him. He just has one leg that's a little shorter than the other. That's where the Special Olympics came in. Stan Simonson is an old friend of mine, and he came up with the idea that if Jeff played with the kids who had handicaps far worse than his own and didn't even have the hope of Dr. Canal, maybe he would develop a better attitude about himself. . . . Not that it was ever bad in the first place, but I . . . I think it's helped. . . ." She trailed off, swallowing several times around a lump in her throat that she thought might be her heart.

Kevin was lost in space as he stood, fondling a bright pink pair of her brief satin and lace panties.

She stared at him for several seconds before

he finally looked up. He had a pensive expression on his face as he slid his long index fingers into the sides of the soft bikini briefs and held them low over her pelvis. His longing sigh told her that to see her in the panties would make his life worth living.

A lewd grin spread across his face. "I love doing laundry," he purred, and watched her cheeks turn as pink as the satin.

Tossing the panties onto the counter and grabbing her up in a tight embrace, he whirled around with her in his arms. Then, taking her shoulders, he held her so he could see her face. "Jan, you are wonderful."

Smiling, she cocked her head to one side and studied him. "Then I don't repulse you because I was married to Tony and kept his name for all the wrong reasons?"

"That he was ever in the same room with you makes me sick. He's the one who's repulsive, not you. In fact, repulsive is the polar negative to the positive forces I feel toward you. You're very special, Jan."

"Thank you," she murmured.

Exhilarated, Kevin was tired of folding clothes and wanted to do something to make her feel the same way.

"Are we about done here?" he asked suddenly. "As much as I adore folding your underwear, dear Jan, I'm ready to move on to bigger and better things." His eyebrows bobbed up and down lecherously.

"Into the boxes and out to the Jeep and we're done," she promised, grinning.

Kevin feverishly started piling stacks of clothes in the boxes. "Great. Let's go back to Smitty's and have a beer and dance."

"But it's Friday night!" she blurted out, becoming anxious again as she picked up a box and followed Kevin, one box under each of his arms, out to the Jeep.

"That's great!" he called over his shoulder. "We timed this just right. They have dancing at Smitty's on Friday nights," he finished, being purposely obtuse.

"But it's been a while since I've been in there at night. I'm not sure what it's like anymore," she warned, her concern growing.

Undaunted and intentionally misconstruing her statement, Kevin's expression turned serious, but his eyes continued to twinkle with merriment. He took her by the shoulders and said encouragingly, "Jan, honey, dancing is like riding a bicycle—you never forget how. And I promise I'll forgive you if you trample my feet."

Walking hand in hand with Kevin down the street toward Smitty's, Jan was filled with misgivings, wondering why she was letting herself get attached to this man. Kevin was most surely a wonderful friend, and she could hope and dream all she wanted to, but they still had no future together. The fact remained, he'd be gone the day after tomorrow and she would not go back to New York.

So why was she so unsure of letting him see what was bound to happen once they got to Smitty's? The tavern's doorway loomed before her, and she felt claustrophobic even though she was still standing outside. Suddenly she was sixteen again—it was her sixteenth summer, when she and Caroline had talked their father into coming to be with them for a week, and she ruined it all by bringing him here. He had strongly disapproved of her behavior. For the entire week he was there he had maintained a stony silence and had cast curious glances her way.

It had been many weeks after that before her grandfather and Sybil had convinced her that enjoying herself at Smitty's was not wrong or evil. They said her father was staid and self-righteous, and that if going to Smitty's felt good to her, it wasn't wrong. She had gone to Smitty's that night. People had been glad to see her and she had been happy and felt good. Weekend after weekend, summer after summer, she had gone back to Smitty's—but she had never told her father.

What would Kevin say? Maybe this would be the test of her increasing attraction to him. Maybe this would make it easier in the end. Then, when he left, maybe it wouldn't matter to her.

She straightened her shoulders and held her head high. A defiant smile on her lips, she passed through the doorway.

* * *

Kevin was bewildered by her reluctance to go to the restaurant. If she had refused outright, he wouldn't have pushed her. And she didn't seem unhappy exactly, just a little . . . distant.

The room was crowded and smoke-filled, and the people were exuberant. Fleetingly Kevin wondered where they had all come from. Since it seemed unlikely that everyone in town would choose a particular day to show up on Main Street, unless it was for a parade, he decided that perhaps the community was a little larger than he had first thought. With not much else to do on a weekend night, this was probably the most exciting place to go.

It seemed that nearly all those gathered here knew Jan. Her name was called over and over again, and she would flash a dimpled grin, raise a hand in greeting or call out a name. People would grab and hug her as she walked by or clasp her hand in theirs and pat it. They told her how glad they were that she had come in, that it had been too long since her last visit. Jan was accepted and well liked here. Kevin was very proud of her, proud to be with her.

Her left hand in Kevin's, she smiled warmly at her friends as she made a way for them to a table. They took a place just to the right of center stage across the dance floor from them.

When they were seated, a barmaid in jeans and a red checkered shirt took their order for two beers. Western music was being played on a jukebox. The room was dark aside from the stage and dance-floor lights and low-lit sconces on the walls dimly lighting the periphery. A candle in a red pear-shaped container glowed on their table. As Jan turned her attention to Kevin, he was bewitched by the sparkling light that cast a mysterious aura to her windblown dishabille. She was a beautiful enchantress weaving a spell of excitement and urgency and she drew him to her like a magnet, his love and desire for her no longer containable.

She placed her hand on the table and he covered it with his. "You are so beautiful," he whispered without preamble, his face wondrous and reverent.

Her lips curved in a tender smile, her eyes warm from the pleasure he gave her. "You make me feel beautiful, Kevin. I've . . . you . . ." She searched for a way to express herself. "I feel so many wonderful things when I'm with you. I—" She broke off in confusion and lowered her eyes, afraid they were too intense, too full of longing. "I've never met anyone like you. I feel so . . ."

They were both taken aback when a large hand landed on Jan's shoulder. Although Jan seemed to know him and smiled at the intruder, Kevin was instantly on guard. *It's a damned beach boy,* he exclaimed to himself, dismayed.

He was tall and blond and tan with rippling muscles and flashy white teeth. He wasn't as tall as Kevin or as virilely built, but he had the strong, lithe body of an athlete and carried himself with an unconscious arrogance that told

Kevin the man didn't get turned down often. Kevin was damned if he was going to leave Jan with this guy prowling around.

Eyeing the invader with suspicion, he noted the hand of ownership on Jan's shoulder. Thankfully Jan wasn't paying it too much attention. As she acknowledged the man's presence, she was friendly but reserved.

"Kevin, this is Stan Simonson. He's the boys' soccer coach and plays with the band. Stan, this is Kevin Toliver of Toliver, Inc., of New York and Denver." She introduced the contenders and there was a firm handshake before the bell for round one.

"I understand you also teach gym at the high school in Boulder," Kevin said, making small talk.

"That's right. I coach football and basketball too. The boys told me about you. They're very impressed with you." Stan's eyes were calculating.

"The impression goes both ways. I'm looking forward to knowing them better. They're nice boys."

"I know. I spend quite a lot of time with them. They're quite a pair." He dismissed Kevin and stalked Jan's body with his eyes in a very possessive manner. "You look great tonight, Janelle. You've stayed away too long." He gave her shoulder a meaningful squeeze.

"Actually it was Kevin's idea to come in. He felt like dancing a little tonight," she told him.

"I don't care how it came about, honey, just as

long as you came." He turned back to Kevin with a sudden thought. "I understand you're leaving Sunday."

Kevin slowly turned the glass of amber liquid that the waitress had just delivered, his eyes downcast. "I'm afraid so," he said. A feeling of despair needled whatever it was in Kevin that kept him from turning his back on a challenge, and he directed his sharp eyes to Stan. "But I still have tonight and tomorrow to look forward to. I plan to enjoy every minute," he said with a meaning Stan couldn't miss.

"Well, I hope you do . . . enjoy yourself, that is," Stan replied. "Janelle, welcome back." He leaned over and kissed her cheek. Kevin's blood caught fire.

Stan moved on to another table, and a short, awkward silence fell between Jan and Kevin before she could think of anything to say.

"When we were teenagers, Stan started this group with a bunch of kids from the high school in Boulder. Smitty is pretty old now and doesn't come here often—his son runs this place. Anyway, Smitty gave Stan and the others jobs here when they were seventeen. They couldn't drink and they had to be home by midnight, which meant the band stopped at eleven-thirty, but it was still a big deal to the guys. Smitty even paid them a little."

Kevin sat watching her talk as if he were memorizing every word. When he didn't say anything, she continued. "This isn't the original band. Only Stan and one other, the keyboard

player, are the same. The drummer is an older
man, a local who joined a few years ago when
Jimmy Donovan moved to Chicago. They have a
new base guitar player, too, except that Larry
Newhouse lives in Boulder and sometimes
comes back to fill in, just for the fun of it." Still
the intense look, but no replies from Kevin. "It's
interesting, sort of, that the mix in age of the
band and the customers works out really well,"
she prattled. "They play some old, some new,
and everyone enjoys it." She paused. "Kevin?"

"Did you come to dance here when you were
young?" He had been listening to her, wondering what she had been like at seventeen, wishing
he had known her then. He felt like he had already missed so much time with her, so much
wasted time.

"Yes, and Caroline came, too, when she was
old enough."

"I wish I'd known you then."

Stan and three other men had gone to the
small stage and taken their places with their in-
struments. A fast, snappy tune Kevin recognized
as a theme song from a recent movie thundered
through the room.

Both Kevin and Jan were distracted by the
start of the music and watched as couples
quickly made their way to the dance floor. The
beat of the song was of the foot-stomping variety, and men and women of all ages were moving forward to do just that.

Although Kevin had become accustomed to
softer music and more refined gatherings over

the years, he was not at all unfamiliar with the sights and sounds before him now. In college and in his earlier years, before money and acquaintances had led him astray, frequenting places like this had been a favorite pastime. There was something about music so loud that you couldn't hear your own thoughts that made your blood burn and your mind relax.

Kevin's hand had remained around Jan's since before Stan's appearance. He grazed the skin on the back of her hand with his thumb, feeling its softness. It was as soft and warm as the rest of her. His fingers could feel the pulse in her wrist as its tempo accelerated.

They sat quietly and watched the varied and diverse forms of the dancers. The song ended and some couples remained where they were, waiting for the next tune, while others returned to their seats.

Stan's rich baritone came over the loudspeakers and the dancers and listeners clapped their appreciation. "Thanks, folks. Thank you." He paused and waited for the crowd's attention. "Tonight's the night, my friends," he said. "We're in for a treat we've all had before and have been wishing to have again."

Kevin glanced over at Jan. Her eyes were closed and she had paled visibly. He was very concerned and leaned closer to ask her what was wrong when Stan continued. "Janelle Harper," he announced.

The overture of a soft, melodious tune started even as Jan turned to Kevin, panic and resignation in her face. Slowly she slid her hand from his and made her way to the front of the stage. The applause and encouragement were deafening.

Nonplussed and burning with curiosity and anticipation, Kevin noted that those people still on the dance floor backed away from the stage and either returned to their seats or stood in embracing pairs eager to hear Jan sing. Jan did not raise herself onto the stage but stood in front of it on the dance floor. A spotlight was turned on her, bathing her sorrel hair with its white rays. The shiny material of her dark green blouse glittered; her skin was pale and perfect. Slowly she moved her body to the rhythm of the heavy beat.

Her emotions were concealed except for the rapid rise and fall of her breasts. Finding a hand mike lying on the floor of the stage, she turned with both arms at her sides, one holding the mike, the other supporting its cord. Her head was lowered, as if collecting her thoughts.

The overture repeated and her head came up proudly. Then, from the beautiful vision before him, came the most extraordinary voice. Her husky tones were clear and pure. It was lovely. She hit notes with a graceful ease that left Kevin awestruck. Her voice was big when it should have been, soft when it needed to be, always beautiful.

Most mesmerizing was the way she sang. She seemed to go totally into herself, and her emotions oozed from her mouth and body in song. She sang about the bewilderment and hurt of a one-sided love affair going bad. Her lover was avoiding her and she was confused and in pain. She lilted the humiliation of begging him to come back, and then cried out that he'd destroyed the dream she had wanted more than anything. In the chorus her body became tense and her hands trembled as she belted out her disbelief that their love was dying.

The music soothed her, as always, and filled her soul. Thoughts of Kevin's disappointment in her shifted to the back of her mind. The song was a favorite of hers, as Stan had remembered, but she'd never felt the story as well as she did now. She thought of the first few days after Tony had left her, then back to the time before she knew why he'd married her in the first place. They were days of confusion, self-recrimination, disbelief, and pain.

She was quaking inside as the song ended and was startled when the applause drowned out the last notes played on Stan's guitar. She smiled her thanks to the familiar faces of her neighbors and friends, but when she turned to Kevin, her expression changed.

Kevin was beaming proudly and clapping vigorously. Before her eyes he stuck his fingers between his teeth and released a loud, shrill whistle.

A slow dazzling grin of great affection spread across her face, warming the core of his very being. At that moment they shared a deep linking of souls that time and distance would never sever. For a moment Kevin thought he saw tears in her eyes, but she turned quickly to face the band.

Stan leaned over to talk to her, and she spoke to him. The tall blond bandleader frowned and argued with her. She seemed insistent and spoke to the other players, who all nodded and smiled at her.

As she turned back, a strain with an upbeat tempo filled the air and she related yet another personalized tale in song. This time she had met a stranger she couldn't forget.

Her graceful body swayed slowly and bumped softly with the rhythm as she warbled her melancholy at not being able to hold the stranger at night, and her conviction that only his kiss, his touch, his loving, could satisfy her.

Hoping beyond hope that this song was dedicated to him, Kevin was delirious as he listened to Jan beseech the newcomer to believe that no one could love him more than she, and that when he was ready to love, he should come to her because she had more love to give than he'd ever need. Kevin believed her.

As this second song came to an end, Jan looked more at ease, and she submitted to the adulation from the crowd. Kevin was ecstatic. She turned and laid the microphone gently back on the stage. As she started to turn back toward Kevin, the band struck up a lively Nashville tune from several years back. Halfway across the floor Stan, who had laid aside his guitar and left the stage, grabbed her hand and whirled her toward him.

Stan apparently asked her to dance, because she looked as if she were explaining something to him. He was cajoling, and Jan looked over her shoulder at Kevin as if trapped. Her expression conveyed her reluctance to leave him alone any longer and asked his forgiveness. He grinned back at her with patient understanding although he was angry with Stan's heavy-handed treatment of her.

She turned back to Stan and began to dance. Her supple body swayed in an easy, fluid motion. Kevin watched as her alluring and very charming form danced in rhythm with the tempo. When Stan took Jan's hand and bumped his hip to hers several times with a teasing grin of encouragement, Kevin grasped the edge of the table to keep from getting up and going after the beach bum.

Timidly Jan bumped Stan's hip in return. With their feet only slightly apart, they bumped hips simultaneously. Reluctantly Kevin admitted it was a graceful expression of rhythm between two people. It also appeared to be a dance they'd done frequently in the past.

Stan raised Jan's hand high over their heads and began very slowly to move her around his body. Other dancing couples stopped to watch. Kevin got the feeling this rite had been performed before since the faces of the observers were expectant and pleased as Stan and Jan never missed a beat without a bump.

Moving easily around Stan's body, Jan bumped his hip and then his thigh with hers.

They bumped shoulders, then Jan flipped around and bumped her other shoulder in the same place on Stan. Behind him, she bumped her right pelvis to his right hip and then the same on the left side. Then she moved around to the opposite side, where she repeated the hip, thigh, and shoulder bumps before coming around to Stan's front. He took her other hand then and held it up to join her other. They thumped pelvis to pelvis each side at a time, then they twisted and struck opposite hips.

The dance continued. It was erotic and grossly sexual. Kevin's body ached as he was forced to watch Jan twist and undulate. Seeing Stan with her, he seethed and became livid, his knuckles white as they clung to the table.

The raucous music came to an abrupt end, and a slow, romantic song started up. Panting and beginning to perspire, Jan thought how good it felt to dance again. Her blood rushed and her heart slammed about in her chest. Smiling at Stan, she said breathlessly, "Thank you. That was fun."

Still holding her hand, Stan's grip tightened. "Stay for one more, Jan," he said, his tone demanding.

"No. I've left Kevin too long. He'll think I've forgotten him." As she tried to pull her hand away he held firm.

"Who cares what he thinks? He's only here on business—he doesn't want your life to stop."

"No. Really, Stan, thank you. It's been fun, but

I'm completely out of breath. I think I'll sit this one out," she said, trying again to pull away.

"Come on, Jan," Stan pleaded.

"This one's mine," a deep, lethal voice said from over Jan's shoulder. Stan's blue eyes met bluer ones that were steely with rage. Stan glared angrily, too, and tried to hold the other's gaze, but he was no match for his opponent. The arrogant tilt of Kevin's head and his tense body told Stan that his rival was no one to cross when riled.

He turned to Jan and with a weak smile mumbled, "See ya tomorrow," then walked back up to the stage to take up his instrument.

Jan would never have imagined Kevin looking like that, nor did she ever want to see him that angry again. She'd seen him amused, bemused, and confused. But anger was a transforming expression on Kevin. He looked dark and evil and capable of inflicting great pain, and it was with some apprehension that she completed her turn toward him.

He glared after Stan until the man picked up his guitar. Then he looked down at her. Jan watched in awe as he became the tender, affectionate man she was used to.

"May I have this dance?" he asked softly.

Without hesitation she moved into his arms. He enveloped her in a strong, secure embrace and they began to sway to the music. The beat of his heart was a steady, familiar, soothing sound. His warm breath tickled her ear and his hand at her back was supportive and comforting, sending little thrills of excitement through her body. His other hand held hers closely near her shoulder, his thumb sensuously caressing her in short strokes. Her breasts, firm and aching, were pressed against his hard chest. When their thighs brushed, it was pure erotica and the core of her femininity throbbed with desire.

The song was nearly over when she raised her head to look at him. Reflected in his eyes were many of the emotions she was feeling—happiness and fear, sadness and panic, arousal and resignation, hope and bitter disappointment.

"Would you like to leave now?" she whispered softly into his ear.

He slowly nodded assent and they turned toward the door.

"Kevin?"

They had walked the distance from Smitty's to her Jeep in silence, their arms wrapped about each other's waists. Had they spoken their thoughts out loud, they might have taken some comfort in their similarity. As it was, they were both disgruntled with the hopelessness of their situation.

The Jeep was still parked in the Laundromat parking lot next to his rented pickup. As they stood between the vehicles, the time for parting had come.

"Kevin," she repeated. He looked down into her face, his eyes clouded with emotion. "I . . . this has been a lovely day. I've enjoyed being with you," she said awkwardly. "But I think I ought to be getting home."

Kevin heard her confusion in her strained voice and understood that she, like himself, needed some time to think and sort out her feelings. He leaned back against the Jeep and pulled her to face him. He slid his long legs out past her on both sides, keeping a firm hold of her with one arm resting on the small of her back, the other toying with a soft red-brown curl at her shoulder.

His hand brushed against the top of her breast. Shock waves of desire rocked Jan and made her tremble.

When he spoke, it was with amusement and a sense of self-realization.

"It's certainly been a day of revelations. You are an incredible woman, Jan Harper. I admit I'm more than a little overwhelmed."

She started to speak, but he shook his head to silence her. "Shh, let me finish." He chuckled softly from deep in his chest. "Wednesday morning my libido went into overload just watching you sleep on my office couch. Can you even imagine the sorry state it's in now?" He shook his head, his eyes twinkling. He looked skyward for several seconds, then back at Jan. "I've seen you vulnerable and very sexy in green silk pajamas," he confessed, grinning at her. "I've seen you at home and comfortable in your cabin and loving and understanding with the boys. I find I've developed a craving for hot dogs and pork and beans, which still has me puzzled. God

knows I'll never view laundry as a chore again"
—he gave a short laugh, teasing her—"and tonight your singing warmed my blood, and
watching you dance with that Stan made me
crazy."

Gently he pulled Jan close to his chest. He
held her firmly against him and stroked her soft
chestnut hair tenderly. "I'm falling in love with
you, Jan," he murmured huskily into her hair.
"Don't tell me it's a stupid thing to do, because I
already know that. And please don't ask me not
to, because I can't control it. Just give me what
you can and a little time to find a way for us to
be together. Something's got to give here, Jan,
but I won't let it be us. I won't lose you now."

Jan looked up into his face, her dark green
eyes brimming with wonder and disbelief. A
gentle smile split her lips, and she stroked his
face tenderly with her hand as if to make sure he
was not a dream. "Kevin . . ." Her whisper
trembled with emotion. "How?" she asked
defeatedly. "Long distance relationships rarely
work, and the idea of moving back to New York
is like a nightmare. I . . . I won't deny that I'm
very attracted to you, but I won't kid myself into
thinking that there'll ever be any more for us
than what's left of this weekend." Her tone was
fateful and realistic, yet it also spoke to Kevin of
her yearning for a solution.

He came forward and gave her a tender kiss
that she would always remember as the essence
of Kevin, of his strength and gentleness, his patience, his love, and his understanding.

"Let's give it a while. We'll think of something," he said, his mouth touching her lips, tenderly at first, then gradually the pressure increased with his passion. Her lips readily parted in encouragement. Her arms came up to twine themselves around his neck. Her fingers dove into his hair to feel the thick crispness of it.

He reclaimed her soft, sweet lips and teased her teeth to open to him. As she invited him in, opening her mouth and pressing into his body with hers, he groaned. Tightening his embrace, he entered to ravish her, to draw the breath of her life into him.

Jan's head reeled as she surrendered to Kevin's power. She felt her breasts engorge and tingle with their need to be touched. Her stomach convulsed, and she felt herself become moist as a slow ache built deep in her loin.

"We'll find a way to be together, Jan. We have to."

Chapter Seven

◆ ◆ ◆

PREPARATIONS FOR TOMMY'S fourth birthday party began early the next day. Before noon Jan had most of the dinner preparations completed and Sybil and the boys had policed the clearing to make sure it was clean and clutter-free.

Finally Jan started her favorite project—the birthday cake. She mixed and baked a layer cake. While it cooled, she started slicing tomatoes and onions. The tomatoes were firm and red and the onions were fresh and juicy and made Jan cry.

That was how Kevin found her when he walked into the cabin. Jan was bent over the worktable in the kitchen, her moss-green eyes red-rimmed and streaming tears. Her nose was pink and she was sniffing.

"Jan. What's wrong?" Frowning, Kevin was all solicitude. He came up beside her and put a comforting arm around her shoulders.

Jan turned to him with a smile on her face. Then suddenly the corners began to droop downward and she took on a most pathetic look.

"Cutting onions makes me cry," she moaned woefully.

He smoothed her chestnut locks and cooed, "Poor baby Jan. Want great, big Kevin to kiss you and make you all better?"

Her face turned up with her lower lip jutting out in a pout, and she nodded an emphatic yes. He looked at her with affection and smiled. His head lowered, and she rose up eagerly.

They met in the lingering kiss they had both hungered for. Her arms wrapped around his neck, fingers playing with the tiny curls at the nape of his neck. He closed strong arms tightly around the small of her back, pulling her into his embrace. They repeated the kiss twice more before standing loosely entwined, gasping for air, and smiling at each other.

"Hi," she whispered.

"Hello," he returned, grinning widely. "Miss me?"

"I must have. I woke up with a decided hankerin' for that kiss."

"Next time, just ask," he teased as he wiped away a delinquent tear. "This wasn't really necessary. I've never had a woman go this far just for one of my kisses."

"It was necessary. It's all part of my plot never to let you walk into a room and find me doing something horribly normal like just standing, or sitting with a book in my lap," she said in self-deprecion.

"Jan, honey. There's nothing normal about

you. You are uniquely wonderful. Don't change anything."

She grinned her acknowledgment and modestly changed the subject. "Where's Hobbs? Did you bring him with you?"

"We met Sybil and the boys outside when we drove up. Hobbs was commandeered into service. He's helping take Sybil's lawn chairs up to the pond."

The old man had been delighted with the invitation Jan had extended through Kevin. Hobbs loved children, but, regrettably, had none of his own.

Kevin had explained his relationship with Hobbs, who had been a physics professor at MIT when Kevin was attending classes there. The two had struck up a friendship. Kevin's company was in the process of expanding by leaps and bounds when it came time for Hobbs to retire. Kevin had begged him to come to New York to be his personal consultant because the man was brilliant on more subjects than just physics. Hobbs might be small and white-haired with age, but over the years he had amassed volumes of knowledge on a wide variety of subjects. Kevin also appreciated his savvy, a talent he had called on many times in the past years.

Professor Hobbs had first moved in with Kevin temporarily while looking for his own place in New York. As it happened, the old man loved to cook, and Kevin could only burn water. Hobbs had a logical, methodical mind, and he was terribly organized. Kevin, on the other hand, had a tendency toward single-mindness, so simple things like eating and sleeping, hiring a cleaning service, and paying bills often took a backseat to new computer prototypes or a new programming scheme. Gradually Hobbs insinuated himself into Kevin's life and became indispensable both personally and professionally. And the old man was happy living with Kevin. He had something worthwhile to keep him busy at Toliver, Inc., and he genuinely cared about Kevin and enjoyed helping him and caring for him.

"The boys asked Hobbs how old he was," he told Jan, who had returned to slicing her vegetables and placing them neatly on plates. "He told them he was old enough to remember when God first made this mountain. Then he went into this long tale about what a mess it had been and what a devil of a time God had had keeping the boulders and rocks from rolling down the sides of the mountain. Tommy was actually struck dumb."

"That's quite a feat in itself," Jan added, laughing merrily as she moved around the big butcher-block table toward the cake.

Kevin followed. Coming alongside her, he dipped his finger into the bowl of icing and popped it into his mouth. "Mmm. What's this, the birthday cake?"

"Yep," she said, playfully swatting his big hand as it swooped down to take another swipe at the frosting.

"And you decorate them yourself," he concluded in admiration.

"Yep," she repeated, "and this one is going to be a work of art. Look." She held up a picture from a coloring book of the Mighty Boarbon.

"What?" he said, frowning in confusion. "You're going to color that and slap it on the cake?"

Jan frowned at him disparagingly. Baffled, Kevin studied the picture, then looked back at Jan, still perplexed.

"I'll surprise you too. Go on up to the clearing and you can see the finished product along with everyone else," she said, giggling. She looked out the window over the sink and turned back to inform him that Gil was already there. "Go pester him for a while and I'll be along later."

Both hands on his chest, she began to back him toward the door. He took another swing at the frosting and with finger in his mouth, eyes twinkling, he dickered, "I'll go if you kiss me."

"You are getting very good at finding excuses to kiss me, Mr. Toliver," she murmured, her ardor in her eyes.

"I know," he stated proudly, folding his arms around her and pulling her close. He kissed her deeply and she returned his urgency with relish. Dropping one last quick peck on her lips before releasing her, he whispered hoarsely, "Hurry."

Kevin followed a well-worn path off to the right and behind the cabins. The woods were dense with Ponderosa pines, aspen, and juniper, and he soon lost sight of the cabins. Another two hundred feet brought him to the famous "clearing."

He had a preconceived notion of what this clearing would be like, having seen what he thought must be clearings in westerns, but this truly surpassed all other images.

In a long oval shape maybe five hundred feet long and four hundred wide, the clearing looked like a field of grass fenced in by towering evergreen trees. The sun filtered through the treetops, its early afternoon heat warming the cozy gap in the forest. There were Rocky Mountain iris and pasque flowers abounding, and the grass was cut short to give the clearing a well-tended, landscaped appearance. In contrast, the woods surrounding the field were completely wild with fallen trees and beautiful blue Colorado columbine spread over the forest floor.

The notorious pond was on the far side opposite the entrance coming from the cabins. The pond was larger than Kevin had thought. Nearly a hundred feet long and half as wide, it was encircled by large flat rocks of various sizes and took on the shape of a huge egg. The original stream flowed into and out of the pond at opposite ends. The water was essentially clear, with only a slight greenish tinge to it.

It was an enchanting place. Kevin suspected that when no one was around, animals drank from the pond, and that at dusk wood nymphs came here to dance.

Today the clearing was buzzing with activity.

"Kevin." His name was boomed out and echoed through the trees. Gil Anderson's large body came ambling toward him.

"Gil," he answered in greeting.

"Come on over and meet my family," the big man said, extending his hand in welcome and friendship.

Besides Gil's wife, there were also Gil's two grown daughters, their husbands and five children ranging in age from six months to nine years. They were a nice, friendly family and made Kevin instantly feel a part of them.

While Gil raved about the various characteristics and special talents of his grandchildren, Jeff and Tommy and three of Gil's grandchildren were jubilantly splashing and kicking about in the pond. Off in the far corner of the field was Hobbs. In all of his aged dignity, he was playing horseshoes with Sybil. It seemed odd to see the old man playing a game in a grassy thicket in the woods, but, then again, Kevin speculated, it was no stranger than the other things he'd seen and felt in the last four days.

Kevin's eyes narrowed, and a frown creased his face as he spied Stan Simonson swaying lazily in a hammock between two trees opposite the pond. He was somewhat gratified to see that Stan had brought a date and reluctantly had to admit the man had great taste in women. The sultry brunette's full head of long, curling hair fell halfway down her back, and her eyes were large and dark, her smile inviting. She had an incredibly voluptuous body that was scantily attired in a red halter and very skimpy white shorts that flattered a pair of long, well-shaped legs.

"That's not going to please Jan," Gil commented in a low rumble. He, too, was eyeing Stan and the dark-haired woman.

"What? That Stan's here? Or that he's here with a woman?" Kevin questioned, digging for the answer he wanted.

"The woman he brought."

"Why?" Kevin asked, unabashed in his curiosity.

"Angela Hartwood is her name, and she's a bit of a barracuda. Some years back she flirted a young man right out from under Caroline's nose. Broke her heart. I heard Jan nearly came to blows with ol' Angie a couple of times that summer." Gil chuckled under his breath. "In a way it was a lot worse to mess with Caroline than with Jan herself. Jan would have shrugged it off, thinking the fella was a shortsighted idiot, but she was very protective of Caroline. Mothered her even when they were little," Gil explained.

"It must have been rough on her when Caroline died," Kevin said thoughtfully, turning back to watch the boys in the pond.

"It was," conceded Gil, his expression taking on the unfamiliar appearance of anger. "And then that bastard of a father disowned her for taking the boys in. . . . I swear, it wouldn't take much more to make me punch that guy. And I'd be glad to do it," he stated vehemently.

Kevin frowned in confusion and in condemnation of the unknown father as he noticed Jan heading toward him and the Anderson family, her tall, willowy body once again clad in jeans that clung to the slight flair of her rounded hips and firm thighs. A bright orange T-shirt tucked in at her small waist accentuated the firm, round mounds of her breasts. Her hair brushed her shoulders and shone with health and cleanliness. Her eyes were lit with happiness.

Jan grinned her greeting, showing off her dimple as she approached the group. "Hi, everyone. What do you think? Is today a great day to have a birthday party or not?"

They all agreed it was. She had come to a halt next to Kevin's chair and, as if unable to keep her hands off him, she laid her long fingers on his shoulder. Looking down into his face fondly, she asked, "Did you happen to bring anything to swim in? I think there's still a pair of my grandfather's trunks around somewhere. I could . . ."

"No. Thanks, but Hobbs took care of that, as usual. He cut off a pair of my favorite jeans and told me it was the best he could do on such short notice."

She laughed softly as she gazed over her shoulder across the clearing at Sybil and Hobbs playing a friendly if sometimes heated game of horseshoes. "Look at them," she said, and giggled. "Frick and Frack."

A more unlikely couple Jan couldn't imagine. Hobbs, frail, dignified, and soft-spoken. Sybil, hearty, earthy, and straightforward.

Coming back to the group at hand, her eyes lighted on the baby in a playpen set up near a long table a short distance from the barbecue pit.

"Is that Janie?" she asked Sara Anderson, who nodded and grinned affirmatively. Jan left Kevin and walked over to the two young couples lounging on blankets near the playpen. With a questioning look at its mother, who smiled her encouragement, Jan bent to pick up the baby.

Holding the small bundle in her arms, Jan played with its hand and nuzzled its neck between comments to the mother. She was both serene and animated. Kevin caught a glimpse of her mothering his child. It was a pleasurable sight. *She* was a sight, a beautiful vision, here in the clearing, where she blended in with and yet stood out from the natural splendor.

Kevin took this opportunity to walk into the woods and change his clothes. He emerged a short time later, just as Jan, standing near the pond, began to shimmy out of her jeans.

Having already discarded the T-shirt, Jan stood beside the pool in an extremely brief blue and green bikini. She was exquisite; she was the mythical nymph. With the forest as a backdrop, her ripe body was vestal to Kevin, and he felt his passion for her stir.

He stood and watched her from the woods. Her husky voice said something to the boys, but he couldn't make it out. Then she turned and without hesitation dove headfirst into the cold water. Kevin turned and moved back into the woods in search of a way to master his body.

Hobbs and Sybil, quietly observing the scene, turned to face each other with raised brows and speculating smiles.

The sun warmed their faces and chests and the tops of their thighs as they floated on their backs, side by side in the smaller end of the egg-shaped pond. Above them an occasional puffy white cloud passed by.

Kevin and Jan had played with the boys earlier. The clearing had rung with peals of glee as Kevin had taken each child in turn and thrown him high into the air only to land, rear end first, in the water.

Exhausted, Kevin had seen the brothers-in-law heading for the pond, towels flung over their shoulders, prepared to swim. Taking Jan's hand he had led her away from the children toward the smaller end of the pool. Reaching out now through the water to touch her, he could feel the heat from her body before his fingers made contact with her upper thigh. She turned her face toward his and gave him a lazy grin.

"I have a confession to make," he said languidly. To her questioning expression he admitted, "I thought J. P. Harper was a man." With a grin of mischief he added, "I'm glad he's not."

Jan laughed softly. "I think J. P. Harper sounds terribly professional." It then occurred to her to ask, "Would you have called me to New York if you'd known I wasn't a man?"

Kevin's eyes grew round in amused in-dignation.

"Are you accusing me of chauvinism?"

"I think so," she answered, grinning.

"I am wounded, Ms. J. P. Harper," he moaned. He clung to the edge of a rock at the far end of the pond and reached out to her.

"Maybe if I'd known who you were, I'd have asked you to come long before I did," he said seductively.

"Would you like to hear my confession?" she asked, her voice husky.

He nodded, his eyes studying her face, wanting never to forget how precious it had become to him.

"I thought Hobbs was you, and . . . don't tell him, but I thought he was probably senile be-cause you had completely ignored the Arizona deal and therefore couldn't possibly have both oars in the water." She laughed, the clear sound filling his head.

Again Kevin mocked her insult with feigned, round-eyed sensitivity. "Jan, how could you pos-sibly imagine me as an old, senile chauvinist?" He shook his head dejectedly, his face sad, as if mortally wounded. "I may never be the same af-ter this. I . . ."

"Oh, wait," she said, laughing outright. "Are we leading up to another kiss here?"

Without a moment's hesitation he pulled her closer, then trapped her between the rock wall of the pond and the rocklike hardness of his body, effectively cutting themselves off from the others at the far end of the pool with his broad back.

Sliding an unoccupied hand through the water, Kevin found Jan's thigh. Watching her closely, he lightly ran his fingers over the top of her leg. Slowly, gradually, he edged closer and closer to the velvety-soft skin of her inner thigh. He watched as Jan tensed and swallowed hard. He held her eyes with his as his fingers glided close to the hub of her womanhood. They dilated and grew darker before his eyes; her lips parted slightly and her breathing began to falter. He could see the pulse point at her throat throb frantically. A slow grin of power came to his face, and his eyes teased her sensuously. "I was thinking of another kiss, but now—" He paused as he moved his fingers higher until Jan trembled convulsively. "Now I'm thinking of other things."

Feeling omnipotent and wanting to drive her a little crazy, he said, "I guess at the moment, though, I'll have to settle for a kiss." He pushed his hand deeper between her legs, curling his fingers around the back of her thigh, and then eased the palm of his hand into her throbbing warmth. When she opened her mouth to gasp, his mouth came down over hers.

Jan's body went limp and began to slide into the water. Kevin moved his hand from her arm down to support her across her back, drawing her closer, pressing her aching breasts against his chest. Her hands, resting against his upper arms, gripped his muscled flesh.

There was no blue sky; there were no trees, no children laughing in the distance. Just Kevin and the sensations he was causing in her body with his lips and hands. Every nerve tingled as he sent wave after wave of electric sensation through her body.

Needing to see her completely vulnerable, Kevin trailed kisses along her jawbone and down the column of her neck until at last he placed one final kiss on the pulse in her throat. He raised his head and held her while he watched her return to him.

Soon she opened her passion-glazed eyes. Her rosy lips were still parted and swollen from his kisses. *She is incredibly beautiful,* he thought to himself.

Eventually Jan's senses returned. She focused her eyes on Kevin's face and gave him a small, tender smile. "Kevin," she whispered. There hadn't been many men in her life, and none she had known had ever evoked such a total response from her. Kevin Toliver was somebody special, and as foolish as it was for him to fall in love with her, it was even more so for Jan to love him, but she did.

Jan lowered her eyes to hide her torment and gather her thoughts.

"Oh, God," Kevin groaned. Jan looked up to see a very unpleasant scowl on his face, his head turned toward the far end of the pond. Following his eyes, she could make out Stan and Angela, who up until now had been keeping to themselves in the hammock. The two of them were now making preparations to join the brothers-in-law, the five children, and Kevin and Jan in the pond.

Suddenly Kevin turned back to Jan, a look of urgency on his handsome face. "Quick. Tell me why he calls you Janelle."

"What? Why?" Jan laughed, confused.

"I hate the idea of that guy knowing something about you that I don't," he said grudgingly.

Jan laughed in delight at his jealousy, then said, "Kevin. Stan doesn't—"

"Please," he interrupted.

"Remember that band I told you about last night? The one Stan started that played at Smitty's and had to be home early?" At his nod she went on. "I was part of it. From June till September, every Friday and Saturday night I sang with Stan's band. I was twenty-one when I stopped spending the entire summer here, but even on my vacations after that they would feature me as the special attraction," she said wistfully. "Anyway, when we first started out we wanted a name. We thought up names like 'Pleasant Valley Strummers' and 'The Denver Devils and the Angel.' They were too much, so we decided to keep it simple with 'Stan and Jan.' But that sounded too rock 'n' roll, and we were definitely country-western, so we settled on 'Stan and Janelle.' Nothing too mysterious," she said, smiling at Kevin and very amused.

"There wasn't ever anything . . . else between the two of you?" Kevin asked hopefully.

"We were friends and we spent a lot of time

together rehearsing, but that's all. I've never even been on a real date with him. And he has never kissed me like you just did," she teased.

"He never will either," Kevin confirmed proudly, but his eyes held a little of the anger she had seen the night before.

"Don't be silly, Kevin. Stan wouldn't think of it. We've been friends for years and he's never even tried," she added, laughing good-naturedly at him.

Rubbing her cheek with the pad of his thumb, Kevin said in an undertone, "Don't you be silly, my dear Jan. He's definitely thought of it and I can't blame him for that. Now that he knows you are no longer the grieving divorcée, he's going to try." Dropping a soft seal of possession on her lips, he whispered, "You be careful."

"Hi. Are we interrupting?" came a sweltering female voice from a few yards away. Angela, wearing a minuscule white bikini, was standing waist-deep in the water. The white set off her bronze skin to a golden glow, and the suit itself set off her other rather enviable endowments as well. Pushing her long dark hair away from her face, she stuck out her chest in what Jan thought was an obvious attempt to impress Kevin with her measurements.

Stan came up out of the water behind her. Putting both hands on Angela's hips, he spoke over her shoulder to Kevin and Jan. "I was just telling Angie about last night. Wasn't it great, Jan? Just like old times, huh?"

"Sure was." Jan smiled politely.

"Maybe we could get together for a few rehearsals and work up some songs. Make it a regular thing again," he suggested encouragingly. "What do you say?"

Still smiling, Jan replied, "I say I'm not seventeen anymore, Stan. I have children and a job that are more important to me now."

Kevin, striving to keep his temper at a low boil, said nothing as he watched Stan and relished Jan's answer.

"I don't think we've been introduced." This came from Angela, who had been eyeing Kevin greedily. "I'm Angela Hartwood. Stan says you work in New York, Mr. . . ." She trailed off purposely, trying to draw Kevin into a private conversation, her eyes darting hungrily over his brawny muscles.

"Toliver," he said simply.

"What is it you do in New York . . . for a living, that is," questioned Angela, undaunted.

"I'm in computers mostly."

"Oh. Is that why you're here visiting? Are you trying to sell Jan a new computer?" she went on, sounding as if she had hit pay dirt.

"You could say that," he replied, his deep voice calm. "I am trying to sell Jan something new," he said with a pointed look at Stan.

"Well, how is it going. Is she going to buy? Or is she giving you a hard time?" Angela purred sympathetically, not realizing she and Kevin were not having the same conversation.

"She's not giving me a hard time at all. In fact, just the opposite. I find her charming," he said with a wink to Jan, who was grinning broadly. Turning back to Stan and Angela, he went on. "As far as buying goes, I think she will eventually. We just have a minor detail or two to work out."

Stan apparently caught the double entendre, because his face took on an angry, sulky look that pleased Kevin. Angela, however, wasn't quite so quick, and with a little double play of her own, she said, "You know, Mr. Toliver, I might be interested in a computer for my own home. . . ." Perplexed, she looked at Jan, who had started with a snicker, progressed to a chuckle, and worked herself into a fit of hilarious laughter. Kevin joined in on the chuckles and was laughing softly with her.

Between spasms Jan started to get out of the pond. "Angie, you are too much!"

Everyone ate to the point of bursting and would have postponed the cake and ice cream until later if they could have been callous enough to put Tommy through the wait. As it was, Jan's cake appeared shortly after the dinner debris had been cleared away.

True to her word, the cake was a work of art. From the coloring book picture, she had outlined the picture of Boarbon on the cake in black frosting. Then she had proceeded to fill in the orange hair that stuck out in tufts around his head. Red lines squiggled through his lavender eyes. His face, warts and all, was a nauseating yellowish-green, and the bright green fangs jutting out from his lower jaw made the cake a perfect replica of the Mighty Boarbon. Kevin was indeed impressed.

"Wow," was Tommy's reaction. Jan beamed at him, pleased that he liked it.

The song was sung, the candles wished on and blown out. The masterpiece was then cut and served with ice cream. When the guests had eaten their fill, Tommy made his way to the gifts, piled high between the lounging, overfed adults, who watched the main event with fond indulgence.

Tommy was enthusiatic over each new gift he opened, but there were definite favorites: the fishing pole from the Andersons, the regulation soccer ball from Stan, and Sybil's hiking boots, which were put on immediately.

Another highlight was Kevin's gift of Delapado the Destroyer, the only action figure Tommy didn't have for his collection. It was also the one Jan had turned Denver upside down looking for.

Sitting Indian-style beside Kevin as he lay on one side with his head propped on one elbow, Jan turned with an accusing look and demanded, "Where on earth did you get that?"

"My sweet Jan, hasn't anyone ever told you that where there's a will there's a way?" He wasn't about to tell her what he'd gone through to get the manufacturer of the action figures to ship him one special delivery. Or that he had been very anxious this morning for fear it wouldn't arrive. After a short pause he added in a voice for her ears only, "I have a definite will, and I'll find a way for us too."

She smiled at him sadly and murmured, "I wish it were possible."

Hearing the discouragement in her voice, he ran his right hand over her back reassuringly. The action was a comfort, but it also stirred her sleeping desire.

"I . . ." Jan started, then frowned hesitantly. "I can't believe what you've done to me in so short a time. I never dreamed that there could be a man like you in my life. When I'm not very careful, I get as hopeful as you sound about a future for us, but . . ."

"But . . ." Kevin prompted.

Jan shook her head and looked away from the intense questioning in his eyes. "I don't know," she groaned. "I'm so torn. So happy and so sad at the same time. My heart says one thing and my head says another. I just wish I had all the right answers for you."

"Look at me, Jan," Kevin pleaded, his voice low, his tone confident. "I know what you're feeling. This has been so quick and so overwhelming and there doesn't seem to be any way for us to be together, but all my life I've followed my gut instincts. They've turned my thoughts and dreams into a multi-million-dollar corporation because I've believe'd in them and they've never failed me."

"Jan," he continued in earnest, "I don't think it's an accident that I've never married. God knows I've always wanted to find a woman I could love who could love me. Someone who would fill me with her laughter, touch me with her passion for life, and share her mind and soul with me." Kevin paused briefly. "My gut tells me you're the one. It's been screaming at me since I first saw you in New York. It's also telling me that there's a solution. We just have to be patient and find it."

Jan listened to his impassioned words and wanted with all her heart and soul to believe them. "I hope you're right, Kevin," she said softly, bending low to press her lips tenderly, trustingly, to his. "I don't know the words to tell you how happy it would make me."

The late afternoon shadows in the clearing, the overfed appetites, and the lull of country-western music from Stan's stereo made the adults mellow and drowsy.

Gil and Hobbs were practicing with Tommy's fishing rod in the pond. Gil's wife and daughters and Sybil sat on a blanket near Janie's playpen talking in low tones. The brothers-in-law were playing a lazy game of horseshoes, and Stan and Angela were again off by themselves in the hammock amongst the trees.

Resting on her elbows, her head on Kevin's hip, Jan wondered about Stan and Angela. They were an odd pair. Jan had no great love for Angela and vaguely wondered if Stan was serious about her. They didn't look like lovers. They didn't touch affectionately, but they had been talking intently and staying off to themselves most of the day.

"Does it bother you that she's here?" Kevin rumbled drowsily. "Gil told me the story about her and Caroline."

"No. I don't mind. It was a long time ago. I just can't figure out what she has in common with Stan," she stated curiously.

"Unless I miss my guess, he brought her here for me so he could have you."

She frowned. "Do you really think so? I was never very good at romantic intrigue. I like things straighforward and honest. It makes things a lot simpler."

"Is that what happened to your marriage to Tony? His dishonesty?" asked Kevin, finally able to put forth the questions he had been wanting answers for.

"Maybe," she said, "but Tony left me. I didn't leave him."

"Why?" He was truly bewildered now.

"There were a couple of reasons. The first, but probably least important, was the boys. He didn't want children. And secondly . . . I guess you could say I just wasn't what he thought I was or hoped I would be."

Kevin sat up, and Jan's head fell on his lap. Scowling, he demanded, "Well, what did he think you were when he married you? Rich?"

"As a matter of fact, yes," she answered with a shaky laugh.

"Well, of all the . . . stupid . . . damned—"

"It wasn't all his fault, Kevin," Jan explained.

"I married Tony for all the wrong reasons. I can't even claim blind love as an excuse. I wanted to—"

"Hey! How about a friendly soccer game?" Stan was suddenly standing above them, Tommy's new soccer ball in his hand.

Apparently while Kevin and Jan had been talking Stan had organized soccer teams. Everyone was playing except Hobbs and Sybil, who opted to watch Janie and the toddlers and keep score.

The teams were divided into the boys against the girls, with a slight deviation in that Tommy and Stan were on the girls' team to make the numbers equal. Stan was goalee for the girls, Kevin for the boys.

The game was fun, full of laughter as the ball was kicked up and down the clearing and into the air for attempted goals. The only two who knew anything about soccer and how to control the ball were Jeff and Stan, so both teams were equally incompetent, which made for a hilarious and enjoyable game.

Suddenly Jan's eyes fell on the portable stereo Stan had brought. Echoing through the open field was Dolly Parton's clear southern drawl singing Jan's song—the song about the stranger and wanting to make him love her.

Jan sought out Kevin's eyes that were gazing longingly across the field at her, exchanging a secret message of love and desire and promise.

Her gaze focused on Kevin, Jan didn't see the soccer ball as it hurtled toward her. Stunning her as it hit the side of her head with enough force to jerk it to one side, Jan fell sideways in shock and landed on her hands and knees.

Kevin was beside her instantly. "Jan. Honey, are you all right? Look at me," he ordered, panic in his voice.

"I'm fine. Just a little surprised," she said with a weak smile.

"Are you sure? The side of your face is all red. . . . Can you see me?"

She chuckled softly. "Yes." Then in a low voice, she whispered, "You're beautiful."

He grinned lovingly, his eyes sparkling like sapphires. "If you can see that well, I guess you are all right. How about you and I sitting out the rest of this match?"

As she nodded, they heard Gil say, "I'm a little worn out myself. My time is beginning to tell on me. Never thought I'd see the day when a bunch of women and little kids could outrun me." He made his way to a blanket and flopped down, groaning. Then Gil lifted his head back off the blanket and addressed himself to Kevin. "I've been meaning to ask you what you thought of this pond," he said with a grin.

"Definitely worth his trouble," Kevin returned. "Actually, if you hadn't told me the story, I would have thought it was a natural pond."

Gil laughed. "If you think the trouble was worth it, you should see what he did when he decided he couldn't live without a waterfall."

Various members of the group snickered and

laughed as if this, too, were a familiar bizarre story about the old man.

"You mean he built a waterfall too?" Kevin asked, incredulous.

"He sure did. You ought to get Jan to take you up to see it before it starts getting dark." Gil's face was amused, as if he knew a good joke.

Kevin looked at Jan and inquired, "How about it? How do you feel?"

Jan exchanged a meaningful glance with Gil and got to her feet. She held her hand down for Kevin in invitation.

"It's one of the wonders of the world. You can't go back to New York until you see it," she said.

"Maybe you shouldn't take me, then," he said under his breath.

The obscure path leading to the falls left the clearing at the far end. It was not as well worn as the trail from the house to the clearing and was overgrown with brush, but Kevin decided that if you knew where you were going, as Jan did, it was definitely a path.

They followed the trail back into the woods several paces before the mountain began its ascent. Climbing became increasingly difficult as they moved higher up the mountain and had to step over fallen trees and large rocks.

Jan traipsed through the forest with the ease Kevin suspected she would have the first day he had seen where she lived. He envied her familiar relationship with the terrain.

Jan watched Kevin's big, graceful body cover

the distance with long, surefooted strides. His tanned skin stood out against his white T-shirt, and his jeans hugged the powerful muscles of his lower torso.

They came to the foot of a large precipice, where the trail ended. Three trees had been cut down and between two stumps was a makeshift bench of weathered two-by-fours. Kevin searched the area and discovered the "waterfall."

Apparently, in the past a crack had formed in the crag and water had run down the wall of rock through the woods to the clearing below. Jan's grandfather must have followed the trail of water up the mountain to the foot of this bluff. Under the source he had made a nearly twelve-foot-tall pile of rocks and small boulders. Close to the top, one rock jutted out past the others so that the water could fall onto the rocks below.

Kevin sputtered in disbelief and then roared with laughter. Weakly he flopped down on the bench and shook his head.

"Your grandfather must have been quite a character. How long did this take him?"

"Years. He'd find a good rock for his waterfall somewhere and drag it up here in a big leather bag he'd made. And, yes, he was quite a character," she said in fond remembrance.

"What was he like? Are there any more of these not-so-natural wonders around?"

"No. This and the pond were his two great follies. He was blunt and gruff and not too affectionate, but then he'd turn around and almost blow himself up trying to create a romantic pond in a clearing in the woods, or knock himself out dragging boulders all over this mountain to make a waterfall. He was very tender inside and although he didn't hug or kiss us very often, Caroline and I always knew he loved us. That was more than we could say about our own father. Grandfather always wanted us to come live here permanently, but that never happened." She paused thoughtfully. "He was also a very wise man, even if he did occasionally do things like this," she said, motioning about her. "I came to depend on him for his advice," she added softly, mourning the old man.

"Why wouldn't your father let you live here?" Kevin asked, extremely curious about Jan's father. She didn't seem to have the best of luck with the men in her life. Her grandfather was dead, her father from all accounts was worthless, and she had had an even less worthy husband.

"I guess that even though he didn't know what to do with us, he didn't want to abandon us completely . . . at the time."

Again there was pain in her voice and now in her eyes as she talked about her father. Who was this guy? What was he, that he could punish his own daughter like this? Kevin was working on some homicidal ideas similar to Gil's.

He stood and gently took her into his arms, where she fit perfectly. Resting his cheek on her head, he said, "You know what I like best about this waterfall?" When he got no answer, he said,

"We're all alone." He ran his hands over her back in a circular motion, tantalizing the skin beneath the thin T-shirt. "Tommy might come up here . . . but he's too busy with all his new things. Jeff won't come because of his brace, and no one else would be dumb enough to trek all the way up here just to see this." He jerked his head toward the pile of rocks. "Maybe that's why your grandfather built it. To be alone."

Jan giggled against his chest. "Why do I feel a devastating kiss coming my way?"

Bringing her face up to his with tender finger-tips, he said, "Because you, my darling Jan, are a very intelligent woman."

Jan felt his breath on her face before his mouth took hers. At first he was tender and soothing. He pulled back and began to nibble on her lower lip and flick his tongue against her teeth, demanding entry. She welcomed him and met his increasing urgency with an unholy force of her own.

He slid his hand beneath her T-shirt and groaned as he felt her cool, baby-soft skin. He ravished her with his hands, but his hunger for her wasn't satisfied. It needed more; it de-manded more.

Kevin ran a trail of kisses over her cheekbone, around her jaw, and then nibbled and teased at her earlobe. Jan moaned as he began to lay soft, sweet kisses along her neck. Her head fell back to expose more of herself to his reverent kisses.

He groaned from deep in his chest, and his eyes came up to search her soul.

"Jan. I have to see you. I need to touch all of you. I want us to make love to each other."

Muted by her own desire, Jan stared helplessly into his blazing blue eyes. Kevin reached out and took the hem of her T-shirt in his hands. Pausing briefly to give her more time to protest, he began to pull the shirt up over her shoulders and head, then tossed it aside. Slowly he pulled at the tie of her bikini top, and it fell loose. Bending over, he placed searing kisses where the bow had been. Then, as he moved to nibble at the soft flesh of her breasts, his hands were at her back releasing the second knot.

Drawing back, he brought the swimsuit top with him. He gazed at her for several seconds and then, as if his fingers might leave a blemish, he softly touched first one breast, then the other.

"Jan, you are so beautiful," he uttered in a hoarse whisper.

Jan's world reeled as Kevin took her breast into his mouth and drew his tongue across the nipple. With his teeth he gently teased it until it stood hard and erect and aching for more. He then moved to her other breast.

When he returned to her lips, he kissed her deeply. Murmuring her name over and over, he showered her face and neck with sweet, hot kisses, then returned to her breasts to draw out wave after wave of exquisite pleasure. She cried out his name as she lost all awareness to everything but Kevin and his touch. As her legs gave way beneath her, he gently lowered her to the grass beside the old bench.

"Jan. Jan," he rasped as he worried the sensitive skin below her ear. His large hand was spread out across the delicate skin of her abdomen. He made her belly quiver as he fingered the skin under the waistband of her jeans.

Jan's heavy arms rose up under Kevin's shirt to feel his sinewy back and his powerful shoulders under the warm, smooth skin.

"Love me, Kevin. Please, love me," she implored.

"I do, Jan. And I will," he said as he flipped the snap and lowered the zipper to insinuate his fingers onto the silken skin of her pelvis and tickle the downy thatch between her legs.

Jan stiffened. Had she heard a twig break? Was someone else here? Instantly alert, she opened her eyes. It took several seconds to locate and focus on the retreating form of a tall blond man.

Kevin felt Jan tense and knew something had shattered their moment. "What is it, honey?" he asked gently.

"I thought I heard something."

Kevin's head rose and scanned the area.

"I don't see anything. What did you hear?"

"I'm not even sure. I . . . I'm sorry," she said, raising her head to lightly kiss his lips. "I wanted us . . . just this once . . . I wanted . . ." She faltered, her body a raw nerve of unfulfillment, her heart too full of love to beat a steady rhythm, her soul an open wound of fear and despair. "Oh, Kevin, hold me," she demanded as she flung her arms around his neck and clung with all her strength and began to cry. "Hold me tight."

Kevin willingly complied to all her demands, while his heart burst and filled him with love and joy and exaltation.

"Shh. Jan sweetheart, listen to me," he whispered urgently. "Tonight may just not have been meant to be, but *we* were meant to be. I love you. I have waited all my life for you. We'll be together somehow. Please, honey, believe me." He held her a little longer, and her sobs subsided as she began to relax again.

Jan drew her hands to the sides of his face and pulled him back so she could see his eyes.

"Kevin, I love you so much. You are so strong and so gentle and kind. I've never met anyone like you. In the last four days you've seen me at my absolute worst, and yet I have never felt so accepted and so loved for being just me. I've never felt so cherished before. I need you in my life. I want to be in yours, and I'm terrified of all that could happen if we get up and walk back down this mountain."

Kevin placed a tender kiss on her lips and smiled all his love for her.

"Don't be afraid, Jan. Please. Nothing will ever change the way I feel about you. Nothing." He confirmed his promise with another kiss. "The answer is simple. I know it is. We just haven't figured it out yet. But we will, you'll see," he said. Standing up, he reached out a hand to help Jan to her feet.

He bent to pick up her clothes while she fastened her jeans. Stealthily he passed his hand gently over her breasts one more time. "As much as I hate to do this, I suppose we ought to get you dressed and go back to the party. After all," he said, calling for a lighter tone of conversation, "there's only so much waterfall to see up here."

Jan giggled. He passed the blue and green bikini top under her breasts as he moved behind her to tie it. Then he tied a bow between her shoulders, laying a kiss beside each one after he had finished. Jan put on her T-shirt.

"By the way," he commented as they started for the path, "you forgot to mention my uncommon intelligence and my unfailing wit and good humor."

Jan's laugh echoed through the trees.

Chapter Eight

◆ ◆ ◆

BY THE TIME they got back to the clearing it was nearly dusk. They found that Stan and Angela had already left, as well as Janie and her parents and their two other children. Gil's second daughter and her family were preparing to take off, also. Gil had waited only to get Kevin's reaction to the waterfall before he made his departure.

Kevin and Hobbs remained to help put the clearing back in order and carry things back to the cabins. While the two men and Sybil had coffee at the big round dining table, Jan bathed and put two exhausted boys to bed.

Jan and Kevin drew out the time to part as long as they could. Finally Hobbs remembered some packages in the truck for the boys, and Sybil, tactfully for once, said good night.

Alone, they looked at each other with the same emanations but with different fears and from different points of view. They were both intoxicated and deeply in love with the other. Passion radiated from their every pore. Kevin hated to leave her even long enough to take the coffee cup back to the sink, but he knew he would be back for her. Jan, on the other hand, wasn't so sure she'd ever see him again. The odds seemed insurmountable that they would ever be together.

"I have to leave early tomorrow. I'm working on a deal to buy a subsidiary of Manning Industries—a plastics factory—and the old goat is giving me a little trouble right now. I have to have dinner with the attorneys tomorrow night to work out some details before I see Manning on Monday. Otherwise I'd try to stay a few more days. Jan, I hate leaving you like this. I don't know what to tell you to convince you that what we have is too big, too alive to die now."

Jan had become extremely pale. Pain was clearly visible in her eyes and in the grim set of her mouth. Not only was Kevin leaving, but she couldn't tell him about Manning Industries, not if Kevin was already getting the runaround with the subsidiary he wanted. He seemed to take for granted that she knew of Manning Industries. Did Kevin know she had once worked for Jeff Manning? Did he know the circumstances under which she had taken her leave from Manning Industries? Obviously he didn't know that Manning was her father. She felt her heart skip a beat. Good Lord, what if her name came up in conversation? Then again, why would it? And there would be time enough after the deal went through to tell him. . . . That is, if they were still hoping for a future together.

* * *

Early Monday morning over breakfast it wasn't Kevin who mentioned Jan's name. The president of Manning Industries did.

"Have any luck with J. P. Harper?" Jeff Manning asked too casually.

Thinking the old man wanted to gloat because he had told Kevin that Jan wouldn't come back to New York, and not caring if he did rub it in, Kevin told him, "You were right. She won't come back to New York." Kevin braced himself for an "I told you so," and was suprised when it didn't come.

"Too bad," Manning said. "She'd have been an asset to you. I didn't appreciate her when I had her." There was a look of shame and regret in Jeff Manning's face that puzzled Kevin, but Manning suddenly launched himself in quite a different direction. "I understand she's adopted a couple of children," he said leadingly.

Curiosity about an ex-employee wasn't unusual, and Kevin had no qualms in relating the boys' relationship to Jan, nor did he hesitate to give Jeff Manning his impression of the boys and their life in Colorado. As he knew Manning to be a kind, generous man, he thought nothing of the man's continued interest and obvious concern for Jan Harper and her two young nephews. After all, she had worked for him for several years, and it was more than easily understandable to Kevin how Manning could have become very fond of her.

Absently Kevin began to wonder just why, exactly, Jan had left Manning Industries at all. She hadn't said anything derogatory when he'd mentioned this meeting, nor had Manning ever had anything faulty to say about her. In fact, it was quite the opposite; he'd recommended her to Kevin and spoke highly of her skills.

Well, it didn't really matter. Jan had had her reasons, and they were powerful enough to make her flatly deny any possibility of coming back to New York. Besides, any fool could see that she and the boys belonged in Colorado.

Kevin sighed with frustration, his mind searching once again for a solution to their dilemma. He wanted to get back to his office to call Jan. He had called her Sunday night after his dinner meeting, but she had found it hard to talk with Sybil and the boys close by. Today he would call while she was working and the boys were outside or at soccer practice. Maybe he could get her to call him again tonight when Sybil was gone and the boys were in bed.

Manning had long since dropped the subject of Jan and the boys, but he continued to ramble on and on as Kevin became more and more impatient to be gone. Maybe the old guy was lonely. It occurred to Kevin that he, too, had found many boring things to say before his thoughts were filled with Jan. How long ago had that been? Last Monday? It seemed like he had been full of Jan forever.

Feeling sorry for the old man, Kevin let him talk, just as he always did when they were together. He'd known Jeff Manning for some five or six years now and had developed a real soft spot for him. Aside from his astute business sense, which he'd shared generously with Kevin over the years, there was something else about him that triggered Kevin's sympathy.

A casual, friendly type of man, Manning always seemed more comfortable listening to others talk about themselves or, like today, discussing financial affairs, politics, sports . . . almost anything but himself. Kevin thought of him as a man who lived in a personal fortress behind thick private walls of loneliness, either unable or too afraid to break through, or refusing to try. Kevin could never decide which.

What Kevin did know of Manning's life, family, and feelings had been years in coming and wouldn't have filled a teacup, but Kevin probably knew more about Manning than anyone else, and he was honored.

Kevin was a busy man, but for the people he was fond of and cared about, his time was free. However, today Kevin entertained a wish that Manning would remarry if for no other reason than good companionship. Besides, Manning had a humor and a sort of gentleness and sentimentality that would appeal to a woman.

Marriage. An intriguing idea when compared to Manning's fate. More alluring yet was the thought of having Jan for his wife—going to bed every night with Jan and waking up every morning to find her beside him. And having the boys around would be great. Kevin had always wanted to be a father, and the boys were nice kids. Maybe later he and Jan could have one of their own. . . .

Kevin's thoughts continued, and so did Manning.

The boys had won their soccer game and were excited and rowdy. As usual, Jan had attended the game to cheer them on. And, as was the custom, she was treating them to a hot-dog-and-ice-cream dinner at Smitty's afterward.

The past five days had seemed like an eternity to Jan. She had spent every minute thinking of Kevin, craving his touch.

Jan poured her energy into the floppy disk project, and now that it was nearly done, a feeling of panic began to rise in her. What would she do to occupy herself to keep from going insane with her need to be with him? She had practically begged Gil for a new project. Although he had nothing to give her for the immediate future, he had apparently heard the desperation in her voice and guessed the cause.

"He's a good man, Jan," Gil had commented sympathetically. "If there's anything I can do to help you two out, just yell. Although my best advice to you would be to move back to New York. Forget about your father."

"How did you . . . Kevin and I . . . how did you know?" she sputtered, embarrassed.

"Jan, I'm not blind. And I've already raised two daughters of my own," he said, laughing at her. "Besides, if you think you're fooling anyone with this busy-with-business act you're putting on, you're all wrong. 'Miserable young woman in love' is written all over you."

It must have been written all over her. She certainly felt as if it were.

Kevin and Hobbs had left the boys' packages on the dining room table Saturday night when they'd left. Sunday morning Jeff and Tommy had opened them to find official Olympic soccer team warmups and shorts and T-shirts inside. Sitting across from her now, they were both wearing the outfits, as they had on Sunday, Monday, Tuesday, and Wednesday.

"You'll be able to stand those things up in a corner at night if you don't let Jan wash them soon," Sybil admonished the boys.

They turned to Jan for confirmation, and she smiled at them indulgently before saying, "It will only take a couple of hours and then you can put them right back on."

She'd have to remember to tell Kevin what a hit his suits were. They talked at least twice a day on the telephone. Kevin usually called by mid-morning, while she worked at the computer in her loft. And she would wait anxiously for Sybil to go home and the boys to go to bed every night so she could call him. He always answered on the first ring, as if he were waiting for her, and she always felt important and loved. Sometimes he would make a second or third call at odd times of the day just to tell her that he wanted to make sure she was still there for him, and Jan's heart would melt and pool at her feet.

"Hello," said a deep voice, jerking her from her reverie. "Great game, guys. I was really proud of you," Stan was saying to the boys, who grinned at the praise. The three of them discussed the game for several minutes, laughing at the highlights and groaning at the mistakes.

Jan hadn't thought of Stan or what he had most likely seen when he'd followed Kevin and herself to the waterfall. Only now did it occur to her to wonder what he must have thought, but it was a little too late as he turned to her with taunting eyes and said, "Heard from your New York friend?"

"I talked to him briefly this morning," Jan replied self-consciously, fibbing about her forty-five-minute call from Kevin.

"How often does he get to Denver? Once a year? Twice?" he asked with a nasty expression.

"I really don't know how often he comes out, Stan." Jan was getting angry not so much at his questions but at his tone of voice.

"Yeah, well, when you get tired of waiting for him to show up," he sneered, "I wouldn't mind walking up to the falls with you." His eyes narrowed as he leered at her, then he flung a "See ya, guys" at Jeff and Tommy and left.

"Whoa! A love triangle," Sybil chortled gleefully. "Wait till Petey hears this," she said, addressing herself to the boys, who looked bewildered.

"Sybil," Jan cried, horrified, "you wouldn't."

"Of course not, dear." Sybil's eyes were alive

with mirth. "But when Petey saw the three of you on the dance floor here Friday night, he became very suspicious. He told me he thought Kevin was going to jump Stan right then and there," she related with relish. "He's been asking me questions all week, but you know I'd never say a word about your affairs, dear."

Jan gasped. "My affairs?"

"What's a love triggle?" Tommy wanted to know.

"It's nonsense," Jan shot to Tommy while holding Sybil with a pointed glare.

That night Jan related the story of Petey's suspicions, omitting the incident with Stan. Kevin chuckled. "I hope the Pleasant Valley poll has me running out front by five hundred votes. I would never be able to hold my head up there again if they thought Stan was the best man for you."

"Well, it doesn't matter how the poll is running, I know which man I want. And it's not Stan," she said, purring the last part over the phone. "Besides, the chances of you coming here again before this all dies down are not too likely."

"Oh, you are so wrong, my lovely Jan," he crooned. "I'm coming back for you very soon. I can't take many more of these phone calls. I have to hold you." His tone was emphatic and full of longing. "If I have to move heaven and earth to get to you, I will."

* * *

The following Friday evening Jan found herself lying on the couch, trying to read a new romance by her favorite author. It was indicative of Jan's state of mind that even romance and passion couldn't hold her attention for long.

On Wednesday Jeff's orthopedic surgeon in Denver had called to say that Dr. Canal in New York had contacted him. Both doctors were optimistic about Jeff's case; however, neither one was willing to guarantee positive results. They would only say that Jeff needed the bone graft no matter what. Whether or not Dr. Canal's experiments would help his leg grow closer to its normal length would remain to be seen. In any case, if she chose to take Jeff to New York for Dr. Canal's experimental program, more blood tests would be required.

At the moment, however, even Jeff's impending surgery was being laid aside for yet another worrisome thought. Something Sybil said at dinner had set off a series of nagging questions and volatile emotions.

Drinking coffee after dinner, Sybil had been talking and Jan, consumed with thoughts of Kevin, had not been listening.

"I sure wish you'd stop that," Sybil had blurted out, finally catching Jan's attention.

"I'm sorry. Stop what?"

"All this mooning around. It's depressing. If you miss Kevin so much, why don't you take the boys and move back to New York?"

Sybil had gone on to talk about how she

would miss her and the boys. Still, love was a powerful force. . . . But Jan had only half listened at the time. Someone else had recently told her to move to New York. Gil—he, too, had made it sound like the obvious thing to do since she was so miserable without Kevin.

Here, in the quiet of her grandfather's log cabin, she mulled over the idea and hoped her old adviser would hear her. She loved Kevin; that much was easy. And it was simple to add that she missed him and wanted to be with him. All points favored a move to New York.

Her job and independence were gratifying. It felt good to know she didn't need someone to support her. She worked hard, did good work, and had a respectable reputation. But she had also enjoyed being vice-president of Operations at Manning Industries, and if Kevin hadn't filled the position, she would undoubtedly enjoy it at Toliver, Inc., as well. Null point.

New York was a big city. There was no reason why two people who disliked each other couldn't live in it and still never see each other again. It had been known to happen, Jan thought wryly. Even if she did happen to run into her father, it would still hurt to be reminded that he didn't love her and no longer considered her his daughter, but she would have Kevin, and his love was all-consuming.

Lastly, the boys—Jeff and Tommy were still very young and children were notoriously good adjusters. They would still have soccer and other sports, school, plus the added advantage of museums and the theater. In fact, the only things they'd miss out on would be hiking and fishing, and they could have those every summer. Then again, there were clean air and open spaces to consider. Hopefully Kevin would offset those, too, by becoming their uncle and giving them added emotional security. They would be a real family.

There were a lot of points to consider, but Jan was leaning heavily toward a move back to New York. She was elated with the idea. Just then the phone rang.

"Hello, sweetheart. Don't you miss me anymore? I've been waiting for your call. You're thirty-six minutes later than usual." Kevin's voice was deep and warm and only mildly worried.

"Of course I still miss you, darling," Jan purred in her most sexy, sultry voice. "Who is this anyway?"

After an hour a curious Kevin hung up the phone and wondered why he continued to tell her things like he'd move mountains to be with her if that was what it was going to take.

Move mountains? Move heaven and earth? Maybe it was a subconscious slip of some kind. Mountains . . . heaven . . . earth . . . Jan? Maybe. Maybe the operative word here was move. Move? Sure, he could move to Denver. Hell, he could move the whole lock, stock, and barrel to Denver. That was it! He would move to Denver!

"Hobbs!" Kevin roared. "Come here and let me bounce a few ideas off you."

One week later, late on a Friday afternoon, an extremely smug Kevin sat in the large leather chair behind his desk. Staring at the couch where Jan had slept less than four weeks ago, he could hardly contain his excitement.

All week long he had talked to lawyers, bankers, stockholders, members of his board of directors, and company department heads. Now, finally, it was all coming into place. The move was tentatively set for September first, barring any major complications. And Kevin couldn't see any right now. They were simply going to move Toliver headquarters to Denver and make the New York offices the eastern division.

"I can't wait to tell Jan," Kevin said out loud, and spun around in his chair like a child.

The plans were all made. He was flying to Denver tonight after Jan's phone call and would be sitting on Jan's front porch when she stumbled out of her bed in the morning. He'd tell her he was moving everything to Denver, and she'd throw herself at him and they'd fall into the grass in front of the cabins. He would ravish her right there. And right there was where he was going to stay.

"Mr. Toliver?" A voice shattered the delectable dream. "Are you all right, Mr. Toliver?" his secretary asked him solicitously.

"I'm terrific, Katherine. What did you need?" he asked, grinning.

"There's a call for you from Denver on your private line. I buzzed, but you didn't answer."

"I'm sorry. Thank you," Kevin apologized. Reaching for the phone, he wondered who it could be. Jan didn't call the office, and she usually called at night. "Hello. Kevin Toliver."

"The wonderful, sensationally sexy, remarkably intelligent, and always good-natured Kevin Toliver? The one who professes to love Jan Harper to death? That Kevin Toliver?" came Jan's voice over the wire.

"That's the one. How may I help you?" He grinned on his end of the line.

"You could meet me at the airport Sunday afternoon, then drive Jeff and me to Children's Hospital and hang around with us for a couple of hours. Then you could take me out to dinner," she informed him.

"I would be delighted to, madam. Are you and Jeff coming for his operation?" he asked, serious now. "They called and accepted him?"

"Yes," was her simple reply.

Kevin sighed, anxious for both Jan and Jeff. "Are you two all right, honey? What are you going to do with Tommy? Leave him with Sybil?"

"We're fine, Kevin. And yes, we are going to leave Tommy here. He'll be lonely, but he'd go crazy trying to sit still in a hospital. Or he'd drive everyone else nuts. In any case, a hospital is no place for a healthy four-year-old," she said.

"I see your point."

"I have a huge surprise for you, Kevin. And don't try to guess what it is," she said in a flurry. "Because you won't even come close. Ever."

"Let me try," he pleaded. "You're bringing a double-barrel shotgun with you because I got you pregnant by osmosis in the pond. So you're going to force me to marry you and live happily ever after."

"Actually, that's about half right," Jan said in a thoughtful voice.

"What? Which part? Are you pregnant? Or are you going to force me to marry you," he asked in mock suspicion.

"Yes," she giggled. Then added, "Wait and see."

"When will you be here?"

She gave her arrival time and flight number and told him she'd already made reservations at her favorite hotel when he asked if he could help by making those arrangements. They exchanged words of longing and love and rang off.

"I wouldn't be too cocky, my dear J. P. Harper. Kevin Toliver has a few aces up his own sleeve," Kevin said to the silence, still very pleased with himself.

At the airport on Sunday an overwrought Kevin shuffled from foot to foot waiting for the passengers on Jan's plane to disembark.

They were nearly the last off, and it flitted through his mind that the airlines usually encouraged the handicapped to get off first. When he saw the sly, teasing grin on her face, he knew she'd gotten off last to drive him crazy. He

winked in acknowledgment of her bad joke and
promised retaliation as he watched Jeff and Jan
walk slowly toward him.

Unable to wait to touch her any longer, he
crossed the twenty feet to her in long, swift
strides. In the most natural way, as if repeated
for the millionth time, they fell into each other's
arms and kissed a long, slow kiss.

"Oh, brother," came Jeff's embarrassed voice.
"In the airport? You didn't say anything about
kissing in the airport, Aunt Jan."

Parting, Kevin slipped his arm across Jan's
shoulder and took her right hand in his so that
she stood slightly in front of him. He felt the
entire length of her body next to his as he drew
her into his embrace. She smelled like wild-
flowers. Still the Jan of Denver, she was wearing
jeans and a pullover cotton knit sweater that
was warm enough for the sometimes cool Denver but still cool enough for the heat of New
York in July. Jeff, Kevin noticed, was wearing
his Olympic warmups.

"Sorry, Jeff," Kevin said sheepishly, "I
couldn't help myself. I think I should warn you,
though, that I plan to be doing that a lot," he said
in a man-to-man tone.

"Well, that's what Aunt Jan said," the boy confessed. Kevin raised his brows in amused in-
quiry and looked from Jeff to Jan and back
again. Jeff continued. "She said that after we
gave you our surprise, you and she would probably kiss a lot. I just didn't think you would start
right here in the airport," he explained.

Kevin and Jan laughed. The spicy smell of his aftershave teased her senses. He smelled so good and felt so warm and strong. Jan knew that whenever she was with him, wherever they were, it would always be like home.

At the hospital Kevin talked and played with Jeff while Jan filled out piles of forms. Eventually the three of them were escorted to Jeff's room. There was another boy in the room, who informed them his name was Steve and he had a broken leg from falling off his grandmother's stoop. The two adults enjoyed listening to the boys talk and get acquainted.

"I already did what you've got. I broke my leg here," Jeff said, showing the place, "and I had wires, too, for a while." He then went on to explain his present situation to Steve, and Kevin was impressed with his knowledge, all due to Jan's teaching, he was sure.

They discussed the fact that Jeff was from Colorado, their families, and brothers and sisters. School was a short-lived subject. It was during Jeff's tale of the Special Olympics games that Dr. Canal arrived.

Tall and thin, he was dark-skinned with black hair and eyes. A soft-spoken man, he talked primarily to Jeff, assuming Kevin and Jan were listening, and made Jeff feel in charge of his own body and very grown-up.

He explained that for the rest of the day the tests would be mostly X-rays and more blood tests, but nothing Jeff hadn't had before. The next day he wanted to take a sample of Jeff's bone marrow. He said he would numb a little of Jeff's hip where the bone sticks out when Jeff was lying flat. When Jeff couldn't feel it, he would stick a needle into the bone and draw out a tiny bit of the fluid inside. Then he proceeded to reassure Jeff, saying that afterward when his hip wasn't numb anymore it would ache a little, like a bruise, but it wouldn't hurt.

Dr. Canal informed Jeff that he wanted to study the fluid, and if it was good, healthy-little-boy bone marrow, which he was sure it was, they could do the surgery on Tuesday and start the drugs on Wednesday.

He called for questions and included Kevin and Jan. Kevin asked about possible side effects from the growth hormone and the doctor reassured them there were very few, but they would monitor Jeff closely. Apparently Jan knew how long they were to stay in New York because she didn't ask, but with the plans to move from New York coming up, Kevin wanted to be sure they would coincide with Jeff's discharge from the hospital. The doctor told him that initially they would remain in New York for two weeks, then go back home in a cast and on medication. They were to see the orthopedic surgeon in Denver once a month and Dr. Canal every six months, until they knew whether or not the procedures were working.

Jeff was taken for X rays and blood was drawn. Then Kevin and Jan sat with him and

Steve until they had eaten and settled in for the night.

Before she left, Jan sat on Jeff's bed and stroked his hair lovingly.

"What do you think, Jeff? Still want to do it this way? Do you like Dr. Canal?" she asked, concerned and understanding of his fear.

"Yeah, I like him. He's got soft eyes."

"Soft eyes?" asked Kevin, who stood at Jan's side.

"They aren't hard or mean. He won't hurt me on purpose."

Jan closed her eyes, aching for Jeff, and held the little boy close.

"What's the number one, most important thing of all time for you to remember, even if you forget everything else?" Jan whispered the question that had become very familiar to Jeff over the past two years.

"That you love me no matter what," Jeff said quickly without embarrassment.

"That's right." She kissed his forehead and then his cheek and said good night.

Kevin gripped the boy's shoulder affectionately and told him to sleep well and that he and Jan would be back early the next day.

Ensconced in a cab, holding hands and smiling knowing smiles, they were both very aware of each other. Jan could feel his presence all around her, in the strong arm across the back of her shoulders and the gentle fingers caressing her arm, in his muscled chest and thigh against hers, in his sweet, warm breath across her face. She felt his mouth close to her face, a mouth that she knew could give such pleasure to her. His eyes were devouring her, blazing bright blue and hungry. The spicy scent of him permeated her senses and filled her with frantic expectation.

The cab was so full of sexual tension that Kevin would not have been surprised if the shaggy hair on the back of the cabbie's head suddenly curled from the heat. Jan was aroused and flushed with excitement. She was regarding him with the lazy, hooded eyes of a seductress. There was a determined, aggressive sensuality about her that both beguiled and excited him.

It was with great reluctance that he finally asked as enthusiastically as possible, "Where would you like to go for dinner?"

"How about your place," she murmured with a sly smirk.

Enthralled, Kevin grinned back.

Closing the door to his apartment, he turned to find Jan with her back to him standing just past the entryway, looking around his living room. He walked past her, suddenly nervous, then turned to face her.

"This is it," he said lamely.

Then Jan gave an absent nod of her head and said, "It's nice. I like it." Reaching out for his gray tweed sport jacket, she began to push it from his shoulders. Her eyes were bold and passionate.

When she had his jacket off and was laying it neatly over the back of his couch, he motioned vaguely with his hands and offered, "Would you like a drink? Are you hungry?"

"No to the first. Very to the second," she said as she reached for and began to loosen his tie.

He grinned crookedly. "My goodness, what's happening here? Where is my shy, reserved, timid little Jan?"

"You left her in the mountains too long," she said seriously. She pulled off his tie by one end and dropped it on the floor.

Kevin watched it fall, and his grin broadened.

Jan went on as she reached for the top button of his shirt. "I am her metamorphosis. I am living proof that you should never kiss and run."

Backing up a step, then another, toward his bedroom, Kevin asked, "Why do I get the feeling I'm about to be ravished right here in my own living room?"

Following forward step by step, she continued her task with his buttons.

"Intuition?" she offered as a possibility.

"Oh, Lord. And I'm out of Mace," he wailed.

"That's too bad," she said with a show of concern as she pulled his shirttails out of his pants.

Kevin stopped in the darkened doorway of his room. He was now genuinely worried and a bit reluctant. "I have another confession to make."

Jan began to glide her hands over his abdomen and slowly up his chest to his shoulders, languishing in the feel of him. The light covering of hair was soft over the hard muscles of his chest.

"You still think I'm a man?" she asked innocently as she began to remove his shirt.

"No." His voice broke with the excitement she was causing, and he chuckled nervously at her reference. "I did something grossly chauvinistic and I'm afraid you'll be angry," he confessed.

"Like . . ." She led him on, dropping his shirt on the floor.

"Like I canceled your room at the hotel and had your luggage sent here instead," he rattled off anxiously.

A dazzling grin slowly creased her face to relieve his guilt. He was instantly self-satisfied and cocky at the success of his grand plan. His eyes twinkled merrily.

Suddenly she sobered and shook her head at him in feigned disapproval. Reaching for his belt buckle, she softly chided, "Kevin, that was a terrible thing to do. In my feminist guidebook that is a definite no-no."

"Oh, yeah?" he countered, sidetracked by what she was doing. He reached out to flick a switch and low, recessed lighting dimly illuminated the room. Flicking a second switch, soft music filtered in.

Jan's mouth dropped open, shocked. "Cute," she accused him as she scanned his lair.

"I just had it installed," he said guiltily.

"Sure," she agreed sarcastically, returning her attention to his zipper. "Does Hobbs know about this? Where is he anyway?" she asked belatedly.

"He said something about the library and a late movie," Kevin said vaguely as he felt her fingers slide between the elastic of his briefs and his taut abdomen. "Actually, I don't think he'll be back. I think he took your place at the hotel."

Jan didn't seem to be listening. "Shoes," she ordered, brushing her fingers along his abdomen, driving him beyond control.

He took another step toward the bed and she followed. Shuffling his feet to maneuver the shoes off, he ground out, "I will if you will." Then he reached for the bottom of her sweater.

Toe to heel, she deftly removed her shoes as he had, raising her hands from his hips to extend them over her head. Slowly he removed her sweater. Biting his lip in concentration, he unfastened the front clasp of her bra and gently pushed the flimsy garment aside and off her shoulders, letting it fall to the floor.

He stood and gazed at the soft swells of her breasts, anticipating the taste of the hard, rosy buds. Hands on her shoulders, he turned with her so her back was to the bed now and urged her backward until her legs brushed its frame. Gently he pressed her down to the mattress until she was lying flat with her feet still on the floor.

With one knee on the bed he tenderly cupped each breast in his hands and brushed the tips with his thumbs. Jan's eyelids slid down and finally closed as her passion and need for Kevin overtook her and she moaned softly.

Deftly he worked the opening of her jeans and stood. Bending down, he took one foot and removed the sock, then reached for the other and removed the second sock. Grasping the bottoms of her pants legs, he pulled them off her in one swift movement. She lay naked on the bed except for a pair of bright pink satin and lace underpants.

He ran his eyes over her possessively for several moments before the pink panties registered. The two lovers' eyes locked, and a slow grin of appreciation for the dream-come-true crossed his face.

"Thank you," he rasped. His throat was tight, and he was finding it harder and harder to control his need for her. He wanted this first time to be perfect for her, but she was so full of surprises tonight, his restraint was fading fast.

His eyes never leaving hers, he bent and hooked his fingers inside the lovely pink silk briefs and pulled them off. Leaving the rest of his clothes in place, hoping they'd help subdue his ardor a little longer, he went to her as her arms opened wide to him in welcome.

Grazing the joining of her thighs with his hand, he moved up over her soft stomach to rest his palm under her left breast. He could feel her tremble, and her heart was racing. He was filled with that same sense of power he'd had at the pond.

"Jan, you are so beautiful," he whispered before his head lowered to take a rosy-tipped nipple into his mouth.

Sharp, aching pains shot upward from the pit of her stomach, and she writhed with the need for her fulfillment. His hands moved over her body, caressing and stroking and discovering all her most sensitive places. His mouth followed the trail his hands had made as he nipped at and kissed her ultrasensitized skin until she thought her heart would stop. She cried out his name and begged him to take her.

"Shh. Not yet, Jan. Soon," he whispered, his mouth moving lower on her smooth abdomen, his fingers separating her thighs and stroking the soft inner flesh.

A delicious darkness fell over Jan, and all she knew or felt were the exquisite sensations Kevin was giving her. She moaned, and her head rolled from side to side as her body began to twist and writhe beneath his erotic assault.

She was flushed and damp with perspiration as Kevin pushed her further into the darkness, where the sensations intensified. Jan cried out as she reached an edge and knew she was going to fall. Kevin gave a final nudge and she fell, plummeting into the cataclysmic splendor she had been seeking.

Kevin held her in his arms as the darkness faded and Jan's world took on light again. Once he was sure she was all right, he left her for mere seconds to shuck his clothes, and then he was beside her again.

Jan watched as he left the bed to finish exposing the perfection of his body. She saw the proof of his manhood, bold and proud. As he came back to her, she vaguely realized what he had done. Her heart swelled to the point of rupture for this man who gave so freely, taking nothing for himself until she had had her fill.

"Kevin," she whispered faintly as she reached out to touch him. He caught her hand and caressed each fingertip with his mouth.

"Shh." He smiled warmly at her. "We'll do it again. This time for both of us." Tenderly he kissed her lips, then murmured, "I love you so much." The second kiss was deep and long and full of his urgency.

He rose above her to enter and fill her completely with one powerful thrust, which she welcomed with an urgent, greedy thrust of her own. They held each other for several seconds, savoring the rightness and gratification of finally coming together. Kevin began to move, slowly at first, but as his control shattered, he became more forceful. He cupped her buttocks with his hands and proceeded to take them both back into the darkness and over the edge together.

Warm and satiated, Jan cuddled deeper into Kevin's embrace.

"Honey, are you all right?" Kevin whispered, concerned. He felt awful, realizing what he'd done to her. He had completely lost himself in her, holding back nothing. If he'd hurt her, he'd die, he thought in shame.

She raised drowsy, luminous green eyes to him. They were full of love and contentment and happiness, but not pain.

"I feel great," she said.

He squeezed her tight and kissed her forehead, then relaxed again. "You're right. You do feel great," he commented.

Tilting her head, she drew her tongue along his jawbone from chin to ear before she murmured, "And my appetite is back."

"What?" he choked. Completely spent, he hoped she meant she needed something to eat.

"Well, you did lure me up here for dinner, didn't you?"

"Lure? Me?" he quoted in innocence.

"Yes, you," she shot back. "What do you call going all the way to Denver to trifle with a lady's affections and besmirch her flawless reputation? What do you call vowing your love and making all sorts of promises and then riding off into the sunset in your own private jet?"

Kevin rose up on his elbow to look down at her, his eyes narrowed dangerously, amusement tugging at the corners of his mouth.

"Well," she continued, undaunted by his implied threat, "I call it luring a lady and then running off before delivering the goods." She smiled.

"Do you know what I call that story of yours?" he asked menacingly.

"What?" Her dimple creased as she anticipated his response.

"I call it too much to bear," he roared as he leapt at her and began to tickle her unmercifully.

She wiggled and squirmed, kicking and hugging her arms to her sides. She giggled and laughed until she was weak and gasping for air.

"If you knew what I have been through the last three weeks, you wouldn't think something like that, let alone say it out loud to my face." He paused momentarily in his torture to allow her to catch her breath.

"You're right," she panted. "I'm sorry. I think I have a reasonable understanding of how you've been feeling," she continued softly, raising a hand to his cheek. "You're right. It wasn't fun and it's nothing to joke about."

His sidelong glance was considering, then he smiled at her indulgently. "Okay, you're forgiven, but you cut me to the quick," he said pathetically.

"Do you need a kiss?" she asked in exaggerated sympathy.

He nodded solemnly, his eyes intent on her face as her arms rose to the nape of his neck and pulled him forward.

Sometime later Jan came out of the bathroom, wearing only the pale blue shirt Kevin had worn earlier. Feeling a little foolish and terribly wanton for her earlier behavior, she realized she had not even seen his apartment when she had come in several hours before.

Jan took inventory now with the jaundiced eye of a homemaker with two small boys. Her face was instantly grim. Only two bedrooms. What if Hobbs stayed? Jan was fond of Hobbs and wanted him to stay with them, but they'd need a bigger apartment.

She groaned as she entered the living room.

Normally she would have considered it a lovely room. It was decorated in earth tones of dark brown and rust, and a comfortable-looking leather couch stood against the outside wall beneath the picture window. Multicolored, coarse-textured material covered the large easy chairs and ottomans that were scattered about. There was a stone wall and fireplace opposite the couch. A wall of bookshelves and concealed spaces, presumably containing TV and stereo equipment, lined the far wall. But the wheat-colored carpet would be permanently black within a week and the wall of glass with the breathtaking view of New York was ridiculously fragile. No one would ever be able to see through the lower four and a half feet with all the fingerprints and dog-nose marks there would be within ten minutes after the boys and Baby move in.

She absently walked over to the shelves and glanced through the titles. Most were technical books, and she was impressed to see a physics book authored by Nathan J. Hobbs. Of course, there were several shelves of Kevin's beloved science fiction paperbacks.

Opening one of the concealed shelves, she found a television on a lazy susan, which pulled out of the compartment and swiveled to any angle desired. Opening another set of doors, she found a sophisticated sound system. Stunned, she did a double take at the cassette tape that had been left inside. A Dolly Parton tape. She removed it, and sure enough, the song about the stranger was there.

Jan half smiled, deeply touched that Kevin had bought this tape. His other tapes were mostly classical, some easy-listening and a few rock 'n' roll. This was his only country-western. She shook her head slowly, incredulous.

"Now this room is perfect." His voice rumbled a short distance behind her. She jumped, startled, and turned to him. "I've lived here for nearly eight years. This room has always bothered me. I couldn't figure out what was missing. An ashtray? A bowl of flowers? A Jan is perfect," he concluded.

She smiled her delight. "Thank you," she said genially, and waved the tape around in front of her to indicate that she was also thanking him for that. She knew she'd never be able to find the words to tell him how much his total acceptance meant to her.

"Hungry?" he asked, then added, "For food?"

"Starving. What would you like me to cook?"

"I'm cooking," he said indignantly.

Taken aback, Jan asked devilishly, "What are we having? Carbon?"

With a withering glance he reached for her hand and led her to the dining room. "Come along, Thomas. You can have your words for dessert," he muttered.

The dining room was a small area in front of the glass wall of the apartment. The kitchen lay beyond it on the other side of an open bar.

Jan smiled tenderly. Kevin had been busy

while she'd been in the bathroom. The table was set for two with flickering candles. Wine chilled in a bucket.

He left her briefly and returned with two plates heaped with food. A second trip to the kitchen produced fresh green salads. Jan was, at first, amazed. They ate filet of sole in a wonderfully delectable sauce she couldn't name, creamed fresh peas, and small new potatoes.

Jan suspected that perhaps Hobbs had cooked the meal, but she said nothing, hoping Kevin would give himself away.

The conversation varied, and they laughed and grew serious in turn. Finally Kevin mentioned the fact that this was the first meal they had shared alone.

Watching him closely, Jan asked, "Does that bother you?"

Looking back at her just as intently, he answered, "Sure, it bothers me. I'm a jealous, possessive man, and I love you. I'd like nothing better than to keep you all to myself, Jan. But because I do love you and because I'm fond of the boys, I accept you as one package. They are part of you, Jan, and you're part of them. How could I care for one and not the other?"

Smiling her relief, she found she had been holding her breath, and let out a long, slow sigh.

"That reminds me," Kevin continued, "I've been wondering how you feel about babies? From scratch, that is."

"Babies from scratch sound wonderful to me,"

she said, a soft expression crossing her face. "I've always wanted to have a baby."

"Me too," Kevin said softly, speculatively.

The meal finished, Kevin began to clear the dishes. Jan stood up to help and he protested, but she was adamant.

The dishes in the sink, Kevin began to rinse them and put them into the dishwasher.

"This sink isn't big enough for the both of us," he protested as she tried to help. He took her hand and led her to another counter across the kitchen. With his hands on her waist he lifted her and plopped her down on the cool flat surface. Back at the sink, he shook his head. "I won't have you doing the dishes on our first night together. Spoils the romantic ambiance. You can do them tomorrow night."

Glancing around her, speculating on where she'd put things when she moved in if Hobbs let her anywhere near his orderly kitchen, she spotted a piece of paper, writing side down, on the counter. Absently she picked it up. She bit her lip and swallowed her laughter as she read Hobbs's note to Kevin on how long to microwave the fish and how to warm the sauce and creamed peas. It even told him where to look for the salads.

Jan folded the note carefully and leaned farther down the counter to stick it into a cookbook.

Having finished the dishes, Kevin turned to Jan with a cocky grin.

"Now, about that dessert of yours," he said, ambling over to her. Jan snapped her eyes closed, bit her cheeks, and took in a long, shuddering breath.

Placing his hands on her hips, his deep voice uttered, "You know, eating crow can be a very bitter experience."

Jan groaned on her laughter and opened her eyes. Her mirth was rioting inside her and was only barely contained in her green eyes.

Kevin insinuated himself between her legs, his big hands coming up to play with the button of her shirt that was fastened between her breasts. "If you promise to be a very good girl, and if you stop making all those nasty insinuations about me being senile . . . and a terrible cook . . ." He punctuated his speech by working loose a button for each negative comment she had made since she'd met him. ". . . I might be able to find something more sweet for you to have."

As he pushed the shirt from her shoulders and leaned over to place sugary kisses at the base of her throat, Jan breathlessly murmured, "Like?"

His hands and mouth were working their special magic on her breasts as he mumbled, "Chocolate cake . . ." His hands went to her hips and pulled her closer to the edge of the counter. "Or vanilla ice cream with fresh strawberries on top . . ." Moving his hands to the tops of her thighs, he began to massage the sensitive inner flesh with his thumbs.

Jan untied the knot that held his velour robe together and, running her hands up his warm chest to his shoulders, she shoved the robe away from him.

Kevin continued his dialogue. "Do you like peanut butter or Oreo cookies?" he asked, pulling her closer still to the edge of the counter so that she had to wrap her legs around him to keep her balance. He kissed her long and deep and passionately. Jan responded to him without hesitation or reservation. When he claimed her, they soared into the darkness together knowing that when they fell into the swirling black hole of ecstasy they would be locked together forever in their loving embrace.

Chapter Nine

◆ ◆ ◆

KEVIN AND JAN were at the hospital early the next morning. Their night of loving glowed in their faces and lurked in their eyes when their glances met briefly and then turned back to the outside world.

Jeff was just finishing his breakfast when they entered. He looked relieved to see them but didn't give away any other indications of his emotional state. Halfway through the morning Dr. Canal arrived to perform the biopsy. Jeff's eyes grew large in his small face when the nurse asked Jan and Kevin to leave the room. She agreed to go but went first to Jeff. Leaning over to kiss his cheek, she whispered, "Remember what you said about his eyes, honey." Jeff looked at the doctor and he must have been reassured, because his fear lessened visibly, although not altogether. "I'll be right outside the door," she said in her husky voice, laying her hand on his cheek in reassurance.

They stood outside in the hallway for what seemed like hours but was actually only forty-five minutes. Kevin propped himself up against the wall with Jan wrapped in his arms, leaning against him.

She remembered the last time she'd been in this hospital. For days she had sat alone watching over both Jeff and Tommy, while worried sick about them, grieving for Caroline, and distracted only by her hurt and anger at Tony and her father. Remembering the loneliness and grateful for Kevin's presence now, she moaned out loud.

Kevin bent to kiss her neck tenderly, taking in her wildflower scent as he did so. "Okay?"

"Mmm." She nodded slowly.

"I've cleared my calendar for most of this next week, but I have to go in for a couple of hours today and tomorrow afternoon and again on Friday. Will you be all right?" he asked, concerned.

"Of course. I'll miss you though," she said.

"Does your going in have anything to do with the buy from Manning?"

"Some," he murmured against her neck. "The old guy talks so much nonsense, I'm having a devil of a time getting him pinned down to a decent price."

"He talks nonsense?" she asked, her tone concerned.

"Not crazy nonsense. Just forever nonsense. He talks on and on for hours. He either just plain loves the sound of his own voice or he's the loneliest man in the world."

Jan considered this news, then said, "I feel sorry for him. I really do."

"Why?" Kevin asked, giving her a curious look.

She smiled into his beautiful blue eyes and said, "When all this is over and your deal has gone through, we can sit and talk. I'll tell you a story about Jeff Manning."

The procedure over and Jeff hardly the worse for wear except for a dull ache in his left hip, Kevin left for the office.

Four hours later he stood in the hospital room doorway and looked inside. Jan was sitting on a chair between the beds, using the other chair as a table in front of her. Each boy had his own table over his lap. They all had a fist full of cards in one hand and a candy bar in the other.

"Go fish," Jan told Steve in a cruel voice. "You are not getting any more of my cards, you little brat."

Steve giggled at Jan's mock anger.

"These boys giving you a rough time, Jan?" Kevin asked, coming into the room and moving over to stand behind her chair.

"Yes," she said angrily. Both boys laughed. "Every time I get three fish, they steal 'em."

"They do, huh? Sounds to me like that's pretty good thinking. Let you do all the work collecting and then steal them right out from under your pretty little nose," he said, giving the boys a comical look of approval. The boys giggled again.

"Where have you been?" Jeff asked. "What took you so long?"

"Well," he drawled, "I had some things to do, which I will explain in a minute. But first you had better close your eyes, because I'm going to kiss your aunt Jan."

Both boys complied, making several disgusted comments. Jan, whose face was already upturned, smiled lovingly at him, and Kevin bent over double to place a tender kiss on her lips. There was a wealth of emotion in his eyes, as with one hand on her cheek he studied her face. Then he straightened up and announced, "All clear."

He stepped outside the room briefly and returned laden with boxes. They spent the next half hour opening board games and trying out the newest line of Toliver portable computer games and electronic toys. They were then divided equally between the two boys.

When the initial excitement died down to a low roar, Kevin left the room again and returned with a square box wrapped in black paper with a big white bow.

Hesitantly he handed the box to Jeff and said, "This finally showed up at my office today. I've been trying to get it since the day after I met you. I had wanted to give it to you at a better time . . . but then I thought maybe you might enjoy it more now."

Jeff carefully opened the box and pulled out a dirty, well-used soccer ball. Written on the ball in black felt pen was, "For Jeff. Good luck and get well soon, Pele." Kevin read the inscription to Jeff, who began to handle the ball with a true reverence. Jeff's eyes were wide with wonder and awe as he looked at Kevin.

"Thank you. It's really neat," the boy said with heartfelt emotion and deep respect. "You were really nice to get me this," he finished.

A slow, affectionate grin spread across Kevin's face. "It was really my pleasure, Jeff. You're a nice kid and I wanted you to know I think so."

Jeff, who had been sitting up in bed, suddenly lurched forward and threw his arms around Kevin's midsection. Not sure what to do, Kevin's hands faltered before they finally fell naturally to Jeff's head and shoulder. An array of new, bewildering emotions flickered in Kevin's eyes.

Jan watched, her vision blurring with tears. She bit her lip as it trembled.

The rest of the afternoon was spent playing games and teasing and laughing with one another. Steve was a delightfully candid boy. He reminded Jeff and Kevin and Jan of Tommy, who was brought up in conversation often.

Dinner was served to the boys, but Kevin and Jan decided to forgo the cafeteria for now and go out for a late dinner once Jeff was down for the night.

It was Kevin's idea, after the dinner trays were removed, to call Tommy on the phone.

". . . And Mr. Toliver gave me a soccer ball that Pele really signed and everything," Jeff was relating to his brother over the phone. There was a pause, then, "I'm not sure where he got it. All I know is that it's mine now. Wait till I get home and show the guys." Then there was another pause. "I don't think we ought to use it cuz the writing might come off. Then it would be just another old soccer ball. See?" Jeff said, explaining.

"Yeah, she's here. So is Mr. Toliver." Looking at the door, Jeff's face lit up. "So is Hobbs."

Everyone turned to see Hobbs enter the room shyly. He smiled weakly, as if afraid of interfering.

Jan smiled warmly at the old man, as did Jeff when he handed the phone to Jan. "Tommy wants you now. Hi, Hobbs." At Jan's stern look, Jeff explained, "He told us to call him just plain Hobbs. He said Mr. Hobbs made him feel old."

While Jan talked to Tommy about what he'd been doing the past two days and he filled her in on all the new gossip, the four in the room conversed in low tones. She also talked to Sybil, then again to Tommy, who eventually asked to speak to Kevin.

With a surprised look Kevin took the phone.

"Hello, Tommy. How is it going out there?" There was a long pause. "I am sorry. You're right. You're much too big to be called Tommy." Kevin looked up and winked at Jan. "Sure. I like dogs. In fact, I've always wanted a great big one. . . . Yes, lots of people have dogs in New York. . . . Well, I never got one because I work too much and don't have time to play with a dog."

As the conversation went on, Jeff and Jan sent glances of impending doom at each other and held their breath.

"Yes. I do like little boys . . . little girls too," Kevin replied, sending Jan a quizzical look before replying to Tommy's next question. "You bet, Tom, if I had a little boy of my own, he would definitely have a dog." Searching Jan's face, he concluded, "No, Aunt Jan hasn't told me her surprise yet. Is it a good one? . . . You won't?" He sounded surprised. "Sure. Talk to you soon."

Handing the phone to Hobbs, he explained, "It's for you." His eyes never left Jan's face as his bewilderment continued.

"Thomas," was Hobbs's salutation.

"Hobbs calls everyone by their long name cuz he says that's what very old people do," Jeff piped in. "He says he never calls Mr. Toliver Kev. I kinda like it when he calls me Jeffrey," he said, and giggled.

Kevin continued to eye Jan curiously, but she was saved an explanation as Dr. Canal came into the room. The biopsy showed Jeff to have fine, healthy marrow. The surgery was all set for nine the next morning. He explained what he planned to do and Jan signed a consent form. He left after answering their questions.

Having finished his conversation with Tommy and unobtrusively listening to the doctor, Hobbs took his leave.

"Will you come again?" Jeff asked hopefully.

"Most certainly, Jeffrey."

The rest of the evening was consumed with preoperative preparation, and Kevin's questions remained unanswered. After the anesthesiologist and a handful of nurses had left, the little boy was ready for bed.

Drowsy from the medication to help him sleep, Jeff didn't put up a protest when Jan kissed him. She told him that she and Kevin would be back early again the next day and that she loved him very much. Kevin and Jan were halfway down the hall when they heard a call-light buzz on. Glancing over her shoulder, Jan saw it was Jeff's and laughed softly.

"He probably needs to go to the bathroom. I'll go help him and save the nurse a few steps. I'll only be a minute," she said as she headed back to Jeff's room.

"Need any help?" Kevin offered.

"No. I'll be right back."

And she was. With a bemused look on her face she told Kevin, "He'd like to talk to you."

Her twinge of jealousy was new, and she didn't relish it. After all, if her dream came to pass, she'd have to get used to the boys confiding in Kevin. Males instinctively shared a certain understanding of each other, and it would be only natural for Jeff and Tommy to seek him out. It all made sense, but it didn't make her feel any better.

The rails were up on Jeff's bed, so Kevin folded his arms on the bars and leaned his weight over the bed to be close to Jeff. There was a look of affectionate curiosity on Kevin's face as he whispered Jeff's name to let him know he was there.

The boy's eyes opened. He was sleepy, but the worry and anxiety were evident.

"I . . . you . . ." the boy faltered, and Kevin waited patiently, encouragingly.

"Aunt Jan told Tommy and me that she loves you a lot," the boy began. "She says you are a good, kind man . . . that you are her friend and can be trusted."

Kevin was too moved to reply.

"Are we friends too?" Jeff asked hopefully.

"I like to think we are."

"Would you do a favor for me then?" he asked, shamefaced.

"If I can, Jeff."

The boy took a deep breath and averted his eyes. With another sigh his story rushed out.

"Don't let Mrs. Silverman put Baby in jail. Me and Gary Spencer dug up Mrs. Silverman's begonias."

Kevin made no reply, afraid that if he stopped biting his cheeks, he'd laugh.

Jeff rattled on. "She's a nasty lady and mean too. We just wanted to get her back. We dug up her begonias when she was in Denver visiting her daughter. We did a good job of it too. We dug with our hands and threw the dirt out between our legs. It really looked like an animal did it. We just never figured she'd blame Baby. But she said he was the only dog around big enough to make such a huge mess."

"I see," Kevin replied calmly.

"The thing is, see, Tommy loves Baby a lot and if I'm not there to tell the real story if the police come after Baby, everyone will think Baby really did it."

"That's true. Why didn't you tell your aunt Jan all this in the beginning? Were you afraid she would punish you?" Kevin asked, curious.

"Yeah. A little. But that's not usually the baddest part about telling her I did something wrong. It's making her unhappy that feels the worst."

"I'm sure it is," Kevin commiserated.

"Sybil says I should think of that ahead of time, and sometimes I do. But I didn't this time. I just did it."

Kevin considered the situation for several minutes before he looked up into Jeff's face. "Tell you what, Jeff. I'll make sure nothing happens to Baby while you're laid up here. And since Baby didn't do it in the first place, it's not likely Mrs. Silverman will catch him trying it again. So we can do two things. We can just forget about it and Jan will never know. Or, when you go home, you can make things right with Mrs. Silverman, like buy her some new begonias. That way, if Jan ever did happen to find out, she'd be very proud of you for taking responsibility for your mistake and doing the best you could to straighten it out."

"How will I buy her new begonias?" Jeff asked nervously.

"You don't need to worry about that till you go home. And then you and I can work something out. Right now you need to get some sleep," Kevin said as he pulled the covers up under Jeff's chin. "And don't worry about it. Or your aunt Jan."

A few minutes later, to Jan's questioning look, he commented, "Nothing important. Just man stuff." His tone cocky, his walk a swagger, he added, "Wanted to know how to make it with the nurses."

"He did not," she stated with shocked vehemence.

"Sure he did. And who better to ask?" He grinned teasingly at her.

"Don't start suggesting anything you don't have time to finish, Toliver," she shot back as they made their way to the elevators.

"Who says I don't have time?" he asked, indignant.

"I says. And I'm hungry."

"Ah. But that doesn't mean we don't have time. I'll take you home. Five minutes to change clothes, thirty minutes to eat—and I'll have time for most anything," he said, satisfied with his schedule. Jan just laughed.

Sitting on the side of the bed in his robe waiting for Jan to finish her shower, Kevin listened to her whistling and singing and recalled the lunch they had shared in Denver and how he had teased her about her unladylike habit. She had told him that her grandfather had always encouraged her to whistle, insisting that people who whistle have happy hearts, that if you were sad and started to whistle, after a while you always felt much better. It had now become a terrible pastime that she had no intention of doing away with.

"Kev-in," came from the bathroom. "Oh, Kev-in."

"What?" he answered, peering through the fog in his bathroom.

"There's something wrong with your hot water. It's starting to get cold," she complained.

"Lord, I hope not. The fog is so thick in here, it'll probably snow," he complained in return, making his way to the shower. "Besides, it's impossible. You'd have to stand in there for days before this building would run out of hot water."

"Well, see for yourself," she said, releasing the shower door.

Gingerly sending a hand inside the shower,

trying not to get wet, Kevin felt the door open farther just before he was yanked in.

"*Jan!*" he shouted, annoyed.

"Kevin," she whispered seductively, flinging wet arms around his neck. She grinned at him with meaning and pulled his head forward for an aggressive, wet kiss.

"Ah, Jan," he said in a completely different tone.

Their loving set their dinner hour back considerably, and a more romantic late-night supper was planned in its stead.

Kevin's choice of restaurants was dimly lit, quiet, and cozy. They occupied a table near the window, where a million single lights in the darkness couldn't outshine the light that shone in their eyes.

As the waiter retreated with their dinner order in hand, Kevin continued his running commentary. Jan suspected he was trying to relax her and keep her mind off Jeff's surgery. It was working. He was charming and delightfully funny.

"How *did* you get that soccer ball from Pele?" Jan asked with great interest.

"Easy," Kevin replied, laughing skeptically. "I have a sales manager who has a friend who does a lot of trade with Brazil, and he has a friend who knows Pele personally."

"You're kidding," Jan exclaimed.

Shaking his head with a silly grin on his face, Kevin went on. "No, I am not. It took me almost a month to get it here. And I practically had to promise my sales manager my firstborn male child, but that's how I got it. I was just relieved he got his name right. I would have died if it came back for John or Jack or Bill." He groaned and raised his eyes to heaven in thanks.

Laughing, Jan said, "Jeff would have been tickled to death with a little dirt from one of the fields Pele has played on. The ball was a real coup. I've never seen him so moved. He's usually so quiet and introverted."

"I'm glad he liked it."

"Thank you for thinking of it. It was a wonderful thing to do."

"Actually, I had ulterior motives." Kevin wiggled his brows lasciviously. "I wanted to make sure I got to you one way or another. The ball has *bribe* written all over it."

"Come on," Jan coaxed, doubtful. "You went to all that trouble just to bribe me into coming to work for you in New York?"

Kevin feigned insult. "If that's all I wanted, I'd have written you a letter, and you know it."

Jan flashed him a heart-stopping grin that expressed her pleasure and contentment, then she murmured, "I guess I do."

She took a sip of wine, watching Kevin thoughtfully. "Have you filled the position yet?" she asked as casually as she could.

"No," he said, watching her in return. "But I do have someone in mind for it."

Crestfallen, Jan put on her best charm-school, cheerful smile. "That's nice."

Their salads arrived and, both famished, there was a lull in the conversation. At last Kevin said, "I've been hearing a lot of interesting things lately."

"About what?" she prompted.

"You."

"Me?"

"Yes." Kevin's face was shrouded in fiendish merriment. "Those boys are little fountains of information."

Jan groaned. "What things have the little fountains been telling you?"

"Oh, it's not so much what they said exactly. It's more like what they said and then didn't elaborate on."

Jan grinned. "I see."

"What exactly have you been telling them?"

"Only that I . . . love . . . you." Jan's voice trailed off as Kevin, looking over her shoulder, began to scowl. "What is it?" she asked, and started to turn to look at what had upset him.

"No! Don't look. Maybe he won't see us. Oh, too late. Here he comes." Kevin sighed in resignation. "Close friends are a good thing to have around, but not when you want to be alone with a beautiful woman. We'll probably be here all night now."

"Toliver. Didn't expect to see you again until tomorrow," came a voice that was painfully familiar to Jan. It drained all the color from her face. Her emotions ran riot, and all she could think to do was to run as far and as fast as she could. Instead, she sat with her nerves screaming, her muscles trembling for control, and her mind numb.

"Hello, Jeff. How are you?" Kevin smiled and stood. He shook hands with the large man who had moved up alongside Jan.

"I see this isn't a business dinner for you either," Kevin commented on the woman standing near Jeff Manning's arm.

Jeff laughed. "All work and no—" He stopped with a jolt as his eyes took in Jan sitting stock-still, eyes lowered, at Kevin's table.

"You remember Jan Harper, of course." Kevin gestured toward her. Something on Manning's face and in Jan's demeanor triggered a feeling of uneasiness in Kevin. Cautiously he watched the two.

After several uncomfortable moments, Manning replied, "Yes. Of course I remember Ms. Harper." He paused, then added, "But I remember her best with a different last name."

Something in Jan snapped. The floodgates opened wide and every emotion she'd felt toward her father in the last twenty-seven years broke through her reserved demeanor.

When she raised her eyes to Jeff Manning, Kevin's lips parted and he gasped silently. Jan's face was grossly contorted, her eyes raw with pain and pure hatred. Her body rigid, her fingers clenched in white-knuckled fists, she looked ready to attack. In turmoil Kevin glanced from one to the other and back again.

Manning had apparently been expecting Jan's

reaction. He looked watchful but relatively unshaken by the encounter.

"It's good to see you again, Jan," Manning said. "Could we have a talk sometime while you're here in town?"

"No," she said flatly, turning away to look out into the night.

The old man sighed defeatedly.

"Excuse us, then. Our table is ready," he said politely, casting Kevin a regretful smile and moving away.

Glancing again at Jan to find her unchanged, Kevin was dumbfounded by Manning's reaction and turned slightly to watch the man walk casually to his table. What the hell was all that about? Kevin wondered as he watched the old man take his chair opposite his dinner companion.

Hoping for some answers, he turned back to Jan. Her chair was empty. Looking up, he saw her bump into a waiter, nearly knocking him off his feet as she charged blindly toward the exit. Kevin threw a handful of bills on the table and followed her.

His concern and fear for Jan dissolved into terrifying panic when he reached the street and Jan wasn't there. Whirling around, frantic for a glimpse of her, he caught sight of her riding away in a taxi.

He met up with her at the elevator doors in the lobby of his building.

"Dammit, Jan. What is going on? Why didn't

you wait for me? Talk to me," Kevin ordered as he grabbed Jan's arm and turned her to face him.

In horror and confusion Kevin took in the expression on Jan's face. It was a mask of sorrow and emotional torture as tears rolled down her cheeks. Crying in anguish and gasping for air, she wailed hysterically, "I hate him! I hate him!" She thumped Kevin's chest once with her fist. "He let her die thinking he hated her. We loved him and he turned his back on us," she accused, and finally began to cry in earnest, a good, healthy, purifying cry. She went nearly limp in Kevin's arms, and he tightened his already tight grasp.

Kevin held her and let her cry, soothing her with his warmth and tender touches. As the storm began to abate, he finally spoke. "It's okay, honey. Let's go up. Everything will be fine."

Chapter Ten

♦ ♦ ♦

BY THE TIME Kevin got her into his apartment, Jan was completely spent. In a trancelike state he deposited her on his couch and went to the kitchen. He returned with two brandies, hers twice as large as his. He held it to her lips and helped her take in the warming fluid. She choked and sputtered but took several good sips before he put the glass in her hands and turned his attention to his own.

Kevin waited while the brandy worked its magical cure on Jan, coloring her cheeks, relaxing her muscles.

"Who is Jeff Manning to you, Jan?" he asked very softly, knowing no mere employer or acquaintance could evoke this kind of response in her.

"My father," she stated in a monotone.

"Jan Manning . . ." he whispered thoughtfully. Bits and pieces of conversations rushed back to him, things Jan had said, things Manning had said, and some of his actions and reactions. Gil and Sybil had told him plenty too. It all came together in the form of a jigsaw puzzle.

It was abundantly clear to Kevin that Jeff Manning had orchestrated this whole thing from the very beginning. He was the one who had highly, and in retrospect too enthusiastically, recommended Jan as a planning consultant. He had apparently assumed that with the quality of work Jan did, Kevin would eventually meet her. Manning's biggest risk was that the two of them would develop any kind of a relationship. The big question here for Kevin was why? What was it all about? How could Manning . . . No, wait. . . . Suddenly it was all *too* clear.

Jan was the estranged daughter and Manning the detestable father, which left Kevin, now partial to both parties, the mediator. "Damn that Manning," Kevin swore inwardly, unable to dispel a grudging respect for the old man's tenacity. Outwardly, his fingers balled themselves into fists to keep from taking Jan into his arms and never letting go of her.

"Will you tell me about it?" he pleaded softly, knowing the pain it would cause her, aware of the price of the trust he was asking for.

Jan was quiet for so long that Kevin thought she might not answer. With mounting concern, he began to fear for her sanity. He was surprised when she finally did speak.

"It wasn't always this way, you know," she said as if she were already halfway through a conversation.

Kevin sat quietly and hoped she would continue.

"When I was little, I remember him calling me Jannie, and we played on the floor and he would laugh when I jumped on his stomach." She took a slow, deep breath. With her eyes fixed on the cold fireplace, her face expressionless, her body limp, she continued unemotionally. "After my mother died, everything was different. He called me Janelle and I never saw him anymore. If I met him in a hallway by accident, he would say 'Hello, Janelle,' but he wouldn't smile at me. When I was six, on my first day of school, I was so excited that I got up early and got dressed so I could see him in the dining room before he left for work. I twirled around in my beautiful new dress and asked him if he thought I was pretty. He said it was a nice dress and to enjoy school, and then he left."

She snorted in disbelief. "That must have been when it all started. I think I've spent the rest of my life trying to please him just once. I never did." She shook her head regretfully.

"My happiness in those days came from the baby that took my mother's place. Caroline. I always loved Caroline and she always loved me. We were very different, but we accepted each other and loved each other.

"I started going out to Colorado to be with Gramps when I was four and I hated it because Caroline was too little to go with me. She was two on her first trip to Colorado and I was six. The housekeeper put tags on our dresses and took us to the airport. My father didn't even tell us good-bye.

"He remarried when I was nine. He must have had his wife custom made, because she hated us. The year after that Caroline was old enough to go to boarding school. So off we went; our step-mother couldn't get rid of us fast enough. That's how we grew up. Boarding school and Colorado in the summer. At Christmas and during spring vacations Father was always conveniently in Europe or out of town. We rarely saw him, and when we did, it was usually because one or the other of us was in trouble. Even after his divorce we led the same life. Nothing changed."

Jan was quiet, recalling the pain and loneliness. Eventually she went on.

"Caroline was so full of life. Tommy reminds me of her a lot sometimes. She hated school, and it seemed like she was always in trouble, especially when she was older. I used to wonder if it was her natural zest for life that got her into one mess after another, or if she did it on purpose to get Father's attention.

"I was never that smart. I tried to get him to notice my scholastic achievements and my honors and awards. Needless to say, Caroline saw him more often in the head mistress's office than I did at award assemblies." She still spoke with no expression as if none of it had affected her.

With each new disclosure Kevin's heart flinched in pain, and yet part of him still couldn't believe this story of Jeff Manning. He wanted to hold her but was afraid she wouldn't finish her story, and she needed to get it out. He waited.

"One time, though, we wrote letters to him all winter long begging him to come to Colorado just for one week the next summer. We wrote from September till May before we finally got an answer. He said he would come for one week. Caroline and I were so excited. We made plans for all the things we wanted to do with him, to show him while he was there.

"That was the year I turned seventeen, the year I joined the band. I was so proud of myself. Everyone said I sang so well, that I sounded so professional. The people clapped and always acted like they enjoyed it. I took him to hear me sing. He left before the end of the first set and for the rest of the week he hardly spoke to me. He just kept watching me like I'd crawled out from under a rock. I wanted to die.

"Needless to say, he never came to Colorado to see us again." She sniffed in self-disgust.

"When Caroline was seventeen, she managed to get more of a reaction out of him than I had. She dropped out of school and married Donald. Father was fit to be tied." Taking on more animation, Jan continued. "I was actually flattered when he called me home to talk some sense into Caroline. I was in my last year of college by then. I talked to Caroline for him, but she said she loved Donald and wouldn't be talked out of it.

"Donald was from New Jersey. He was a freshman at NYU. He wanted to be a schoolteacher—an elementary-school teacher, because he loved children. He was a very nice person, and I liked him a lot. But Father said he wasn't good enough for Caroline, that he was only after her money and that he'd prove it by disowning her. And he did. Disown her, that is. He never spoke to her again.

"I was so angry at him for that. He hurt her so badly." Jan's voice cracked with emotion but then grew stronger with her ire. "I finished school and applied for a job at Manning Industries. I worked my fingers to the bone and gradually earned my seat at his executive table. In the four years I worked for him, we only talked business, even socially. At the office I called him 'Mr. Manning' and he called me 'Ms. Manning,'" she said with a satisfied nod and then, as if to emphasize her anger, she added, "I remember he even had the nerve to show up in my office— several times, in fact—trying to find out about my life and Caroline's as if nothing had ever been wrong between us. But by then I'd had enough. I told him just to stay on his side of the desk. If he couldn't make up with Caroline, he needn't bother talking to me," she stated vehemently.

"Then Caroline got pregnant with Jeff. It was an accident, but they were both thrilled. At first Donald tried working and going to school, but when they were expecting Tommy two years later, it got to be too much, I guess, because Donald didn't finish his junior year. They were happy though. Except about my father. Caroline wanted him to know his grandchildren, her babies. She even named Jeff after him as a sign of her love, hoping he'd forgive her. She sent him a birth announcement and didn't get any kind of response.

"Donald got a job in a factory upstate. When Tommy was born, they named him after my grandfather, who was very pleased with the honor." Jan released a long, torturous sigh and turned to look at Kevin. Her smile was weak, but she looked more like the old Jan. She pulled her feet up off the floor and tucked them under her. Then she laid her head on his shoulder and said, "This is about when Tony comes in. Do you want to hear all that too?"

"Let's get it all out tonight. We'll bury it once and for all," he said, taking her into his arms at last. He kissed the top of her head as she began again, still wondering if they were talking about the same Jeff Manning.

"Tony was a junior partner in the law firm that handled all my father's interests. My father had taken a liking to him, but when he eventually approached me for a date, I couldn't really think of any good reason not to accept. After all, my being the boss's daughter wasn't common knowledge. He was very charming and showered me with attention, but there was always something about him I didn't like. I didn't trust him. I did, however, delude myself into thinking I could learn to love him. Over the months he became more ardent and started talking about our future together. And then suddenly he wanted to get married right away. At the time I really thought we could have a wonderful future together, so we eloped one afternoon and got married. There was a week in the Bahamas for a honeymoon, then we both went back to work. Instead of being pleased, my father was furious. Tony said he literally gave him the cold shoulder. I found it hard to believe my father could hate me so much that he would do that to his precious Tony. But with everything that happened after that, I guess I was wrong.

"We had been married exactly two weeks when I got the call from the police. Caroline and Donald had been killed in a car accident and both boys were injured and in the hospital. It was a nightmare. There were people everywhere wanting to know about funeral arrangements and who was going to take responsibility for the boys and their care. I called Tony and asked him to come help me, but he said hospitals and death made him uncomfortable, that he couldn't handle situations like that, but that he'd call my father for me and let him know I needed help." Jan shrugged, then went on.

"Thank God there was a will. I'll never understand what possessed Caroline and Donald to write one. It wasn't exactly something I would have thought was at the top of their list of priorities." She shook her head as if still puzzled. "Anyway, I was the boys' guardian and had gained custody. That made things at the hospital a little easier, but I still had all the funeral arrangements to make. I . . . I called my father for advice, but he was unavailable at the time, and he either never got the message or he didn't care, because I did it all myself," she said sadly, even as a note of bitterness crept into her voice. "I have to give it to him though, he played the part of the grieving father real well at the funeral. He came and sat at the back of the church. He looked awful and I almost felt sorry for him until he tried to say he was sorry. I told him the person he needed to talk to was gone. It was too late to be sorry," Jan said on a note of sorrow and exhaustion that seemed to radiate from deep within her soul.

"When I got home from the funeral to change clothes before I went back to the hospital, I found Tony's note. It said that he had no intention of living with two sniveling little brats. And now that my father had disowned me for taking in Caroline's kids, I was of little use to him and I could handle the divorce any way I chose to."

"That bastard," Kevin snarled. "I ought to wring his neck."

Jan chuckled softly, warmed by his protectiveness. "That's exactly what I wanted to do to both of them, but actually it was the best thing that ever happened to me. I was so hurt and angry at them, I think I hit bottom. I was truly relieved that Tony was gone. And I had had it with my father. I didn't care if he'd disowned me. I didn't even care if I never saw him again. I quit my job that same day and made arrangements to move to Colorado. When the boys could travel, we left, and I have never regretted for one minute making that move, nor have I spoken to my father."

Leaning back so she could see his face and gauge his reaction, she said, "I'm sorry for the way I reacted tonight; he caught me off guard. I honestly thought I could come to New York and not relive it all. I truly thought my life was so full of love and happiness now that his evil couldn't hurt me."

There was a frown of troubled confusion on Kevin's face. Knowing both Jan and Jeff Manning, the story he'd just heard created a jumble of conflicting impressions in his mind.

"I want to know why you didn't tell me Jeff Manning was your father. Was that a test or something to make sure I wasn't another Tony Harper?" Kevin asked impassively.

"No. Not at all. At first it didn't matter because I thought you only wanted me to take the job. Then when I realized you knew him, I knew you couldn't be another Tony because you already had as much money as my father has. And you also knew I had two boys and was working to support us. When I discovered you didn't connect me with him, I kept silent because I didn't want to ruin the subsidiary deal for you. If you had mentioned me to my father, he might have made things much worse or called it off completely. I was going to tell you after your deal went through."

Kevin sighed and held Jan possessively, as if his doubts had the power to tear her away from him. He was torn between the man who'd been his good friend for several years now and the woman he loved but had known for only a short five weeks.

Even though Jeff Manning had used Kevin to get to Jan, Kevin also knew him to be a gentle, sensitive man who, in his eyes, couldn't possibly have done the things Jan spoke of. Jeff had admitted to hurting his daughter, but that he could have done so in such a heartless, cruel way didn't seem possible to Kevin.

Jan, on the other hand, had a boundless capacity for loving. It was in her nature to be understanding and forgiving. That she could intentionally torture an old man by depriving him of her affections and that of his grandsons didn't seem conceivable either.

As the seconds passed Kevin could feel Jan waiting for some sort of response from him. That she was in pain he couldn't deny. He wanted to console her, but he needed to be honest as well.

"Jan," he uttered softly, pressing a kiss into her hair, "I don't know what to say to you. Are . . . are you sure you haven't gotten the wrong impression somewhere along the way?"

"It's a little hard to get a wrong impression when your father disowns you," Jan returned, bewildered by Kevin's skepticism. "I remember it distinctly. It happened the day after my sister died and the day before my husband left me, sort of sandwiched in there between a couple of major emotional disasters in my life," she finished cynically as she turned in Kevin's arms to face him.

Eager to be tactful, Kevin tried again. "But did he really? Did he actually say it in so many words?"

"Yes," Jan stated emphatically, "in just those words. I'm not an idiot, Kevin. I know when I've been rejected by my father," she said, growing angry and defensive at his questioning. "Tony's letter said my father had disowned me for taking Caroline's children. It seemed par for the course at the time."

"But I can't even imagine him doing something like that, honey," Kevin tried to explain. "I've known him for years, and I grant you he's a very private man, but I think I know him as well as anybody and he's not capable of that kind of . . . of cruelty."

"So what does that make me? Some sort of neurotic little rich girl with an evil-father complex?"

"Of course not," Kevin said, frustrated, as he felt the warmth of her body leave him and watched as she began to pace the room furiously. "It makes both you and Jeff victims of a gross misunderstanding."

"Misunderstanding hell!" Jan shouted back at him. "The only reason I was halfway civil to him after he disowned Caroline was so that I could try to mend the misunderstanding between the two of them. When he did the same to me, it became abundantly clear that I'd been a fool. He didn't want anything to do with either of us.

He'd just been looking for a reasonably good excuse to be rid of me as well."

"What about all the attempts he's made to talk to you?" Kevin threw the question in her face as another point to consider.

"What about it?"

"What if he has an explanation or he's changed his mind and wants to be forgiven? Why haven't you at least listened to him?"

"Why should I?" Jan was becoming angrier by the minute at Kevin's defense of her father. "It wasn't my idea to sever the relationship, such as it was, and there can't possibly be a reasonable excuse for what he did to me or to Caroline and the boys. So rather than upset my life and the boys' lives with having to deal with his interruptions, I just don't deal with him at all."

"Maybe you should," Kevin suggested, getting to his feet. "Honey, the man would give his right arm just to talk to you. He'd give both arms if you'd forgive him. At least give him a chance."

"A chance?" she exclaimed. "He's had chance after chance since I was four years old to show me that he loved me, he wanted me, that he needed me in his life. Would one more chance make any difference?"

"It might."

Jan was silent. Her eyes narrowed slightly as she studied Kevin with great deliberation. At the moment it was easy to forget how much she loved him; she couldn't see the man she'd trusted, the man who she thought had accepted her so completely, who would support her and comfort her in times of need. All she could see was another man she'd placed her faith in who was now betraying her in favor of his friendship with her father.

"What are you doing?" Kevin asked as Jan turned and walked away from him toward the bedroom.

"I'm leaving."

"Why? Where are you going?" He followed her to the doorway, a frown of concern creasing his face as she took up her suitcase and began packing.

"To a hotel—where I should have gone in the first place. You'd think I'd learn," she muttered with great self-derision.

Kevin stood watching her. "That kind of goes for both of us. I should have known you were too good to be true," he said, his voice cool and hard, his disappointment in her obvious. "You're not the woman I thought you were, Jan Harper. I thought you had courage taking on the boys and building your own life and business out west. But you're really just a runner. You ran away with the boys, all the way to Colorado, just to avoid your father. And now you're running from me because I can't agree with your decision to be heartless and vindictive to an old man. I thought you were human and vulnerable and made mistakes like the rest of us and that you'd understand the same imperfections in others. I thought you were a woman who could love someone forever, a woman with compassion and forgiveness. . . ."

Jan had turned to face him by now and was taking his every word as a dagger through her heart.

"I guess I was wrong," Kevin finished sadly.

Jan trembled and reached out for a nearby chair to keep from crumbling into a mass of tortured human flesh.

"It's too late to go to a hotel," Kevin said in an emotionless monotone. "Stay in here tonight— I'll sleep in Hobbs's room. You can run away in the morning if you want; it'll be more convenient then."

And with that he closed the door, taking Jan's heart and spirit with him. Numbly she sank into the chair too spent to cry, too hollow to be angry, too empty to feel anything but . . . empty.

By seven the next morning Jan was again at Jeff's bedside. The boy was quiet and apprehensive, but his front was brave. Almost as brave as Jan's.

The night hours had been long and lonely, wretched with memories and raw with self-doubt. She hadn't even bothered to sleep as Kevin's words played themselves over and over again in her head, accusing, but never offering a solution.

The next two hours seemed to race by. A nurse came in and gave Jeff a sedative. The medication worked and soon Jeff's eyes grew heavy and he closed them.

Kevin arrived to find Jan holding Jeff's small hand in her own as she watched the young boy sleep. Guilt welled up inside him as he took in her pallor and the lines of stress and fatigue. He'd picked a lousy time to goad her into facing Jeff Manning. With young Jeff's surgery uppermost in her mind, she certainly hadn't needed the extra tension, but he couldn't change the circumstances.

"Hi," he said in a loud whisper as he advanced into the room.

Jan looked surprised to see him, which stung a little but was to be expected, he decided.

"Hi," she returned almost inaudibly. "I didn't think you'd be here. I . . . you weren't home when I got up, so I thought maybe . . ."

"What? That I'd avoid you until you went back to Colorado?" he questioned, guessing at her thoughts. The expression on her face told him that was exactly what she'd believed, so he smiled and reminded her, "That's your game, Jan, not mine. I came to see how Jeff was doing."

Jan turned away, biting her lip.

A short while later a stretcher was rolled into the room. The attendant picked Jeff up off the bed and laid him on the stretcher. The boy didn't stir; he was sound asleep. Jan kissed him and stroked his cheek, trying to transmit her love to him.

"You got someone inside there?" a burly, middle-aged man asked. He was slouched in a corner chair in the surgical waiting room. Wearing a plaid shirt and tan work pants, he had been watching Jan as she nervously whipped through ancient periodicals and watched the clock.

"Yes," she said, her smile weak. "My little boy."

"Something serious?" he asked with real concern.

Jan considered the question for a minute before she answered. "No. Not really. I guess it could be something a lot worse. They're doing a bone graft on his leg."

"It's always hard to see little people laid up though," he said, commiserating.

"Are you waiting for someone also?" Jan asked in return.

"The wife is having a hysterectomy. We have seven children. You wouldn't think she'd care, but she was pretty torn up," he confided.

"I'm sorry," Jan said helplessly. "I hope she'll be all right."

"Old Sadie is a bouncer," he said jovially. "She'll be fine." He paused, then went on. "You know, you and your husband there should treasure your time together now. Me and Sadie were so busy working and raising kids that when all this come up, it made us realize how much time we've wasted when we could have been enjoying each other. We just figured we'd have forever. It don't always work that way."

Kevin and Jan simply looked at each other, then at the man.

"You are absolutely right, sir," Kevin agreed.

Time went by and several more people came into the small room to wait. Jan and Kevin sat side by side, counting the minutes. Both were anxious for Jeff and both took comfort in the other's presence, but they were a million miles apart.

Over and over Jan continued to deny Kevin's accusations from the night before. She wasn't a runner; she was a survivor. Leaving New York had been a way to cut off the painful memories that had threatened to destroy her. And God knew she'd wanted to understand and love her father, but there was only so much rejection one person could take. Why should she expose herself to that all over again? How could she take the risk of exposing the boys to that kind of heartache?

Granted, their family circle was small with just herself and Sybil. Having a grandfather would be nice for the boys. It could even be wonderful if he could love them. Was she wrong in denying them this opportunity to meet the great Jeff Manning? Could it all have been a misunderstanding, like Kevin thought? Could her father hurt her any more than he already had? Did she owe him the time to speak his piece just because he was her father? Jan sighed heavily in indecision.

"You know, the hospital puts the slowest clocks in these waiting rooms," said their friend from the corner. "They want you to think you're getting your money's worth in there."

Jan and Kevin smiled at him and his attempt at levity. Jan looked up to see Dr. Canal at the doorway looking for her.

"The procedure went very well. Now it's just a matter of medication, diet, and time to tell if it will work," the doctor told them after he had shown them into a smaller room across the hall. He went on to explain that the first three or four days were the worst as far as the pain went, and that Jeff would be likely to sleep during most of the next twenty-four hours.

Soon after their conversation, Jeff was returned to bed and checked by the nurses before Kevin and Jan were allowed to see him again. He was pale and drowsy, but he smiled at Jan when she whispered his name and tenderly kissed his forehead, then he drifted back off to sleep.

"I think I'll go back to the office," Kevin declared quietly a few minutes later, when it became obvious they had nothing to say to each other. "Can I get you anything before I go?"

"No. Thank you," Jan said, finding it very difficult to look him in the eye. "I appreciate your being here though."

Kevin nodded his understanding and, without a second glance in her direction, left the room.

The light faded in Jan's hazy world and her conscience began to nag at her once again. With Jeff asleep and his roommate in physical therapy, Jan had nothing better to do than listen.

What if Kevin was right? What if her father truly did love her and she never gave herself the chance to find out? As much as she had wanted to, as hard as she'd tried, she never really had been able to hate him. She was angry and hurt, but she had always wanted her father to love her as much as she loved him.

So maybe it was best if she did give him one more chance. If he didn't come through for her and the boys this time . . . well, Kevin could adopt the aging executive.

Jan jumped in startlement as a hand fell gently on her shoulder, disturbing her deep thoughts.

"I'm sorry, Ms. Harper. I didn't mean to frighten you," Hobbs said with a small, gentle smile. "I stopped by to check on Jeffrey. How is he doing?"

Jan returned his smile fondly, answering, "He's fine. Very drowsy and in considerable pain when he's awake, but he just sort of drifts in and out. The nurse says he'll remember very little of today, and by tomorrow he'll be a little better."

Hobbs nodded, looking at Jeff with deep concern etched in his wise old face.

"I thought perhaps, if you'd allow me, I could sit with young Jeffrey while you took a break," he offered kindly. "This must have been a great strain on you. You look a bit tired."

Jan knew she looked more than a bit tired, more like she'd gone to hell and back on a skateboard. And she felt worse.

"Actually, Hobbs, you're a blessing. There's nothing I'd like more than a rest right now, but I have a very important errand to run. I'm not sure how long it will take, but if you could stay with Jeff until I return, I'd very much appreciate it."

"I will be happy to stay," he replied sincerely.

A short time later Jan felt like Dorothy knocking on the wizard's palace doors, full of apprehension and hope, reluctant but desperate as she pressed her father's doorbell. Suddenly she was ten years old, fussing with her hair and straightening her attire, wishing she'd worn a dress instead of her comfortable old jeans.

The door swung open and there he was, tall and silver-haired. His gray-blue eyes took in every inch of her in disbelief.

"Jan." Jeff Manning finally spoke, and then in an uncharacteristic vent of nervousness added, "Come in. Come in. You're early. I hadn't expected you for a while yet, but I'm glad you're here. Please—please come in."

Jan moved into the large penthouse suite that had changed little since her childhood. There was a quiet elegance about it that over the years still reached out and made her feel at home again.

"Should I have Dottie bring in coffee or would you prefer something stronger?" her father asked politely, and Jan could almost feel sorry for his obvious discomfort and anxiety.

To anyone else Jeff Manning would seem only courteous, but Jan knew him better than most people did. He kept his hands in his pockets and looked at her frequently, searchingly. His normal manner was far more casual and much less awkward.

"Nothing for me, thanks," Jan replied, refusing to show her own agitation. "I didn't realize you were expecting me."

"I wasn't," he said with a wry smile. "Kevin was."

"Kevin was?"

"He said you'd come. In fact, he bet me his life you'd be here before six, and it's just now four-thirty," Jeff told her with a perceptive chuckle. Then noting Jan's confusion, he explained, "He may be my friend, but you're the one he loves. He was here at the crack of dawn this morning calling me everything from a son of a bitch to a pigheaded fool and madder than I've ever seen anyone to be. Told me if I didn't settle things between us and make you happy that I'd have to answer to him. Please, sit down," he said, laughing softly. "He apparently said some things to goad your better instincts that he's afraid you won't forgive him for."

"I see," was all Jan could say, not sure she liked being manipulated in such a hurtful way, or in any way at all.

There was a long pause as father and daughter studied each other, unsure of where to start mending the rift between them.

"I . . ." Jeff started thoughtfully, "I find I have a lifetime of sins to make up to you for, Jan. Your lifetime anyway, so maybe I should start in the beginning and go along as best I can."

"All right," Jan said softly, easily, sensing something very new in her father.

The old man sighed. He suddenly took on years and looked very old and beaten. "I didn't . . . I didn't set out to hurt you, Jan. Or Caroline either. I do love you, I just . . . I . . ." He faltered, searching for a way to explain. Finally he started over. "Please, there's so much I need to say. Let me explain and then we can talk if you like. Just let me say this, okay?"

Jan nodded, clasping her hands in her lap, truly wanting to listen.

"There was only one other person in the world I loved more than my daughters, and that was your mother. She was so beautiful and so full of life. She filled my entire universe. You were her pride and joy. She had wanted you more than anything else. We had trouble conceiving, and the pregnancy was just one complication after another. But you were finally born, beautiful and healthy. We were delighted. And you were delightful. For three years the three of us were the perfect family. And your mother and I were content with just you. We lived for you."

Misery washed over Jeff Manning's face as he recalled what happened next.

"Olivia got pregnant again. The doctors advised her against going through with the pregnancy, considering the difficulty she'd had with you. I myself didn't think I could watch her go through it again. But she was so optimistic. She said she'd had you, and you were so perfect and wonderful that we would have double the pleasure with two children. She wanted to have the baby.

"When she held Caroline in the hospital, she was ecstatic. She said that having given birth to two such perfect, beautiful baby girls was probably the only reason she had been put on earth because she'd never done anything else so grand. Two weeks later she was dead."

The devastation he had felt then was still fresh for Jan to see. He was silent in his grief for several minutes before he remembered Jan and continued. Jan's heart wept for him empathetically, wept for them both.

"That was when our world went sour. And it was most definitely my fault. I turned away from my daughters and into myself in my grief. You look very much like your mother and you meant so much to her. So many of my memories of my wife featured you, too, that to look at you was a torment. Caroline too. Olivia gave her life willingly, happily, just to give birth to Caroline. I resented her and loved her at the same time.

"I buried myself in my work. The less I was home, the easier it was to live, to survive. Your grandfather tried to help. He took you in the summer, and Caroline, too, when she was old enough for the nanny to take her. Later, the housekeeper would take you both to the airport and I would watch as the stewardess took you to the plane. I couldn't bring myself to kiss you or hug you or tell you good-bye. Something in me always wanted to, but the pain would come and wash it away.

"Later, when I remarried, Gloria suggested boarding school for you girls."

"She hated us," injected Jan matter-of-factly.

Jeff Manning frowned in concern and reflection. "She said you would learn all the polite, social, feminine things little girls were supposed to learn from their mothers. When I suggested she teach you, she said she adored my girls, but she'd never been very good at communicating with children. I detested the idea of sending you away and procrastinated for a long time. Finally I decided that maybe Gloria was right. You girls certainly were not getting much from me, and Caroline was turning into a little hellion. She needed some discipline that I couldn't bring myself to give her. I thought I would at least try it, and if it didn't work, I could always bring you home. Maybe get a governess or something." He paused briefly and looked her straight in the eye. "Was Gloria ever cruel to you?"

"Just indifferent. I don't think it was worth the trouble to her to be mean to us," Jan told her father with a careless shrug.

Jeff considered his daughter for several seconds before he continued. "Well, anyway, the two of you girls seemed to thrive there. I called the headmistress often to check on you. Caroline, they said, did well in her classes, but they did from time to time have problems with her 'high-spiritedness,' as they called it. They described you as well mannered and quiet. They said you were exceptionally bright and doing very well in school. I thought at the time that I had made a good decision."

A tone of regret crept into his voice as he continued his monologue.

"A pattern developed over the years. I spent my time wrapped up at the office, and you girls shuffled back and forth between boarding school and Colorado. I never saw you except for an occasional visit to the school to get Caroline out of some scrape or another. At one point your grandfather wanted you to stay permanently in Colorado with him. He said my girls were miserable and that if I didn't want them, he did.

"I did want you, Jan, and I loved you. All that time I kept telling myself that the pain would eventually pass and I would make up for all the time we spent apart. We would be a real family again.

"Then one year, out of the blue, the two of you started writing hordes of letters to me asking me to come to Colorado that summer to be with you. I sometimes got two letters from the same girl in one day. I thought maybe the time had come when I would be able to be a father to my daughters. I wanted at least to try. The first night I was there you took Tom, Sybil, Caroline, and me to hear you sing in town. Do you remember that? I know I'll never forget that as long as I live."

"I embarrassed you by singing in public, didn't I?"

"Of course not. Is that what you thought?"

"Yes," Jan replied defensively.

Jeff Manning closed his eyes in regret and failure. "You sang beautifully. Like a nightingale. I
was very proud of you. But as I watched you, I
saw you. You were a beautiful, graceful, full-
grown woman. Not the child I had come to
make up with. You were a stranger with your
own mind and goals and . . . you didn't need
me. You didn't need a father anymore. I was too
late. I had waited too long. And it was all my
own fault. I went home feeling worthless, de-
feated, and full of remorse. Not only had I failed
my daughters, I had betrayed the trust my wife
had in me."

He laid his hands, palms up, on his knees in a
gesture for Jan's understanding.

"I was lost. I didn't even know where to start a
conversation with either of my children. They
were adult strangers. The next thing I knew, Caroline had dropped out of school and was getting
married. She was only seventeen. She hadn't
even finished high school. She was going to
marry that kid from New Jersey who was still in
school; they had no money, nothing. I was so
unskilled at talking to you two by then that I
couldn't make her see reason. In a last-ditch effort to call her bluff, I threatened to disown her.
It didn't even faze her." He shook his head.

"So you disowned her," Jan said, her voice
laced with bitterness.

"Of course not. I only threatened, and she assumed she was. What was I supposed to do then?
Knock on her door one day and tell her it was
all a sick joke?"

"What about when she named Jeff after you?" Jan persisted.

"I was thrilled and terribly flattered. But again I was at a loss for words. What do you say to a near stranger who names her firstborn after you? Thanks?" Jeff Manning asked, frustrated with his ineptness to communicate with his own daughter. "I made provisions for the boy in my will . . . and later for his brother, too, but I didn't know what else to do. What do you send an estranged daughter who does you such an honor? A silver spoon? Blue booties? I racked my brain." He threw his hands up in a sign of futility.

"Now you, you were a different story and a different kind of failure," he started absently. "I knew you'd finished college at the top of your class, but you didn't invite me to your graduation. I assume it was because you thought I didn't care, which wasn't the case at all. Then you showed up in personnel at the company and applied for a job. You didn't claim me there either. You listed your sister as next of kin, and from all reports that got to me, you denied any relationship between us. At first that hurt, but when I realized you could have gone to work anywhere, I thought maybe you just wanted to make a place for yourself in the company without my help. And I respected you for it, and I let you be." He shook his head once again before he continued. "You did good work, too, and I was very proud of you. I promoted you rapidly, but it had nothing to do with nepotism. You had an excellent grasp of the business world and realistic values, and you never settled for second best. I was truly impressed with you, our relationship, such as it was, notwithstanding."

Jan's father sighed in retrospect, then forged on. "But even after you got to the executive board, I found we couldn't talk or get to know each other. The times I tried, you had me shut so far out we could hardly talk about business, let alone our relationship. Even when I broached the subject of Caroline and tried to explain, you cut me off cold . . . not that I blame you. I knew you were angry and hurt for your sister as well as yourself, but I became extremely frustrated trying to reach you. Then Tony Harper entered the picture and another of my best-laid plans blew up in my face," Manning said sarcastically.

"I admit he had me hoodwinked. I thought he was a bright young man with a promising future. When he started seeing you socially, I was actually pleased. Shortly after that I started receiving hints of caution from friends and close associates about Harper. Finally I had him investigated. It turned out he was a . . . well, I'm sure you know now what he is. When I found out, I went to him and warned him to stay away from you. It was my fault he caught on to our relationship in the first place. I had such confidence in him, I told him one night at dinner who you were and how proud I was of you." Manning's self-condemnation was clear in his voice and on his face.

"The next thing I knew, you'd eloped. I didn't know for sure how much he meant to you, but I knew what you meant to him, and again I floundered in helplessness. You know," he said thoughtfully, "I consider myself a pretty shrewd businessman. But when it comes to handling anything personal or as important as my daughters, I've been a bumbling idiot."

He went on to give an example. "When Caroline died, I seized at what I thought was the perfect solution. I thought that if I continued the deception of the feud with Caroline and refused to acknowledge her children and disown you if you took them in, I could scare Harper off. You and Caroline were always as thick as thieves. I knew you'd never give up the children. So when Harper called to let me know that you'd assumed custody of the boys, that's what I told him, and sure enough, he cleaned out your accounts and took off. I tried to tell you the next day at the funeral that we needed to talk, that you didn't have the whole story about Harper. I wanted to meet the children and help you in any way I could, but you'd already jumped to the same conclusion your sister had. You wouldn't speak to me, and short of causing a scene right there, there wasn't anything I could do."

"Why didn't you come to me before that? Or after the funeral, when we could have been alone?" Jan asked with growing amazement at the way their lives had gotten so far out of control.

"I had a call to go out of town on business. I

had intended to confess everything to you and beg your forgiveness when I got back and after you'd had some time to cool off. I never dreamed you'd up and quit your job after he had cleaned you out, or that you'd pack up and move the boys and yourself to Colorado before I returned."

"What about before the funeral, after the accident, when I could have used your help?" she asked pointedly, recalling the loneliness she'd felt at the time.

Jeff Manning leaned back in his chair and gave Jan a hard look. Then he said, "I hope you never have to know the death of your own child, Jan. I hope you never have to carry the burden of guilt at having failed that child and the knowledge that making it up to her was gone forever." He paused, then answered Jan's question. "If I couldn't go to her, be of use to her when she was alive, what good would I have been to her in death?"

"It would have been a comfort to me," Jan indicated in a soft voice.

The old man was pensive. "If I had thought that at the time, I would have been there."

"But . . ." Jan frowned, perplexed.

"But what?" Manning encouraged, his voice gentle and curious.

"Tony said he'd call and tell you that I needed you and . . . and I called the office myself and left a message. . . ."

"Jan. Honey," he beseeched her, "if I'd known there was an opening that wide available to me, you have to believe I would have walked through fire to get to it," he said adamantly, then added, "I didn't get the messages. I'm sorry."

Both became silent and speculative, each tangled in their own thoughts and emotions. It was a long time before Jeff finally broke the spell.

"Jan," he said, using her name as a plea, "I know I've neglected and abused every right I ever had as your father. I know I've hurt you. I've never been a demonstrative man and I . . . I tend to keep my thoughts and emotions to myself and now, too late, I've realized that because of the way I am, I've lost all that's precious to me in life.

"Maybe if I'd known Caroline better and trusted her judgment, I could have seen what you did—that Donald and an early marriage were right for her. If I'd taken the time to know you, I could have told you directly about Harper and saved you a lot of pain. I have a thousand maybes and hundreds of better solutions to the way I dealt with you and your sister over the years, but they're of no use to me now," Jeff Manning said despairingly. "I know a lot of water has passed under the bridge between us, Jannie, but . . . well, if you could find it in your heart to forgive me and give me yet another chance to show you how much I truly do love you, a chance just to get to know you . . . I would be so very grateful," the man finished humbly, his eyes searching and pleading with Jan's so intensely that she finally had to lower them.

"Can I have some time to think about what you've said?" she asked in a quiet voice, afraid to make a purely emotional decision, wanting to throw her arms around her father but feeling gun-shy.

"Certainly," he conceded, grateful already that she hadn't flat out refused him as he had expected. "But . . . I think I should explain one more thing before you go."

Jan was silent, her head and heart full of remorse for the part her own pride and stubbornness had played in this calamity.

Jeff Manning took a deep breath. Making confessions didn't come easily to him. "When I got back from Europe and found you gone and later discovered that you'd had your marriage annulled and declined to take my name back, I knew . . . I'd lost it all. My woman, our babies, my grandchildren, everything." His fists balled in his lap. "If that old saying about it being darkest before the dawn is true, that's where I was. In the darkness. In the darkest time of my life." His voice was low, his eyes downcast. Then, purposefully, he sat up straighter and said, "Young Toliver was my dawn, Jan. I used and manipulated him almost as badly as I have you, I'm afraid, so please don't hold his part in all this against him."

"My relationship with Kevin isn't really any of your affair," Jan told him quietly and not unkindly.

"You're dead wrong there," Manning said with

a smile, pointing an index finger at her for emphasis. "I set the two of you up," he declared, eyes twinkling as Jan's brow furrowed. "Actually it was a double-edged setup and a lot of it was left to chance but, like I said, I was desperate.

"I've known Toliver for years. There isn't a phony bone in his body, and he's scrupulously honest in all his dealings, both personal and professional. I knew that if I could get the two of you together somehow, I could use Kevin to plead my case to you at the very least. If things worked out the way I hoped, which apparently they have, the two of you would hit it off and then I could make up—in a way—for siccing Harper on your trail. So I very carefully maneuvered him into hiring you for his western division and left the rest up to fate. This time, thankfully, the gods were with me. When Sybil told me—"

"Sybil?" Jan interrupted, surprised to hear that name in this conversation.

"Ah . . . yes, Sybil. I've . . . I call Sybil and she keeps me informed on everything about you and the boys," he told her sheepishly, then chuckled uneasily. "She thinks we're both a couple of stubborn fools."

"She would," Jan confided with a wry half smile, not caring and almost grateful for Sybil's sympathetic spying.

Manning nodded his agreement and returned Jan's knowing look. "When she finally told me that Kevin had shown up on your doorstep and that you two were rapidly falling in love, I knew it wouldn't be long before he found out about the two of us. When he did, I knew, too, that he'd either defend me as his friend or he'd come looking for my blood. Turned out he did both, but the result was what I wanted . . . what I needed. You're here and we're finally talking."

"What if it hadn't worked?" Jan's voice was quiet, awed as she was by the tremendous chance her father had taken. "What if this day had never come to pass?"

Manning, too, was aware of the risk and could only shake his head in wonder.

Father and daughter sat silently for several minutes, measuring and calculating the other's perceptions.

Finally Jan moved to leave. "I need to get back to Jeff," she said awkwardly, "but . . . I'm glad I came today."

Jeff Manning smiled his heartfelt thanks and watched as she stood to leave. Rising to his feet beside her, he couldn't quite suppress the grin he felt all over as he asked, "What are Toliver's chances of getting out of this unscathed?"

A teasing sparkle came to Jan's eyes as she looked up at her father. At that moment she experienced a deep thrill that touched the child, the adolescent, and the mature woman in her at sharing a small pleasure with her father.

"Fifty-fifty," she calculated with a grin. "It'll all depend on how nicely he grovels."

"Could I . . . come by and look in on Jeff in a few days when he's feeling better?" he asked tentatively.

Jan considered this, then said, "Yes, I think so."

Chapter Eleven

◆ ◆ ◆

JAN RETURNED TO the hospital to relieve Hobbs of his charge and to discover that she'd just missed Kevin's visit. She and young Steve entertained each other quietly throughout the afternoon as Jeff floated in and out of consciousness.

He would whine in frustration from the pain and drowsiness and Jan would soothe him with cool hands and a reassuring voice before he drifted back to sleep.

The dinner hour came and went, as did Steve's bedtime. Eventually Jan was left alone in the dimly lit hospital room with two sleeping boys and her own private thoughts. She contemplated the fragility of human relationships and how easily they could be destroyed. That the presence or absence of a single word or action at any given point could strengthen or weaken a bond between two people had been made very clear to her that afternoon.

How could two people like Jan and her father, who professed to love each other and who wanted and needed each other's love so much, flounder about in such close proximity for so many years and never connect? And yet on a fluke Jan could travel two thousand miles to meet Kevin and form such a perfect, instant bond.

"Hi," murmured a low, deep voice from the doorway. "It's getting late and I started to worry," Kevin said as he moved into the room.

Jan kept her back to the door and closed her eyes in relief and happiness at the sound of his voice. How she loved this man who in less than six short weeks had come to know her better than anyone else in the world . . . better than she knew herself.

Taking her stillness as a bad omen, Kevin approached her cautiously. "When I was here earlier, Hobbs said you'd gone off on an errand. Was it anything . . . interesting?"

Jan bent her grinning face toward her chest and shook her head.

"Oh," was Kevin's deflated rejoinder. "How is he doing?" he whispered, taking in Jeff's pallor, his motionlessness, and the huge cast on his leg.

"He wakes up in pain from time to time. Then they medicate him and he goes back to sleep. Poor baby. I hate seeing him like this."

Kevin nodded in agreement. Walking over to check on Jeff, he laid his big hand on the small boy's bony shoulder. He could feel a heart beating beneath the frail ribs. A big, loving heart for such a little boy.

Silently Jan moved up behind him so that when at last he turned to her, their faces were mere inches apart. Automatically Kevin's hands reached out for her. She looked haggard and drawn with fatigue. Tired as she was, however, her smile was radiant as she looked up into Kevin's clear blue eyes.

"Thank you," Jan said, just barely above a whisper.

"For what?" Kevin returned guardedly.

"For being you. For loving me and having faith in me. For knowing that I'd never be truly at peace within myself until I at least tried to reconcile with my father. And for being an extremely cocky little busybody," she finished with a teasing glimmer in her eyes.

"An extremely cocky little busybody?" he questioned, feigning indignance with an arched brow.

"Well, don't you think that you were being a little presumptuous last night, saying all those horrible things to me and then just taking for granted that it would all work out and that I'd forgive you?" she asked curiously.

Kevin laughed softly. "Believe me, sweetheart, I didn't for a second take that for granted. All those things I said last night are true . . . except for that last part. I knew I wasn't wrong about you, I just thought maybe you'd been so busy lately taking care of everyone else that you might have lost touch with the real Jan."

"What if I hadn't taken the bait?"

"Then I was going to go after your father for hurting you so badly and so deeply that he'd destroyed your ability to forgive," he stated simply, pulling her a little closer.

"Would you kiss me and hold me for a long, long time," she requested, suddenly exhausted now that the whole world was right side up again.

He drew her to him, his arms strong and supportive, possessive and comforting. Safe and secure cradled in his embrace, Jan knew she was protected from all outside forces. She could hear his heart hammering slowly, steadily, inside his wide, muscular chest. He kissed the top of her head and an electric current shot through her body. Kevin raised her face to his and gave her a tender, loving kiss. Slowly the kiss ended and Jan searched his eyes for any lingering discord between them. All she saw was her love for him reflected back at her.

"Does this mean you and Manning have settled things between you and I can come out of the doghouse now?" Kevin asked, cherishing the feel of her in his arms once again. It had been a long twenty-four hours.

"You can come out," Jan muttered into his shirt, soaking in his body heat and growing drowsy. "As for my father, I don't know. I went there half hoping I'd get the chance to claw his eyes out, but when I got there he seemed so anxious and sincere. And he talked to me more than he ever had before. And . . . I think I understand him a little better, but it's going to take more than an hour's worth of words. It's going to take time and effort on both sides before things ever become right between us." She paused briefly. "I wish he could have talked to me like that twenty years ago. Things could have been so different," she said wistfully, stifling a yawn.

Kevin gave her a reassuring squeeze and pressed a kiss of promise to her temple. "Come on. I'm taking you home. We'll let the nurses know, and they can keep an eye on Jeff."

They went home and Jan made western omelettes for a late dinner. Over coffee they made a call to Colorado. Sybil and Tommy wanted to know all about Jeff's operation and in return filled Jan in on all the Pleasant Valley gossip. Tommy begged Jan to come home soon because his grandmother had cooked him lima beans for dinner that evening.

Together they cleaned up the dinner dishes. Both Kevin and Jan had surprises they were eager to reveal, but they mutually refrained from discussing their future together until things with Jeff settled down and they could give their full attention to each other and their plans to be together. So they talked about other things. Gradually talk turned to the office.

With a sheepish look Jan reluctantly asked, "I've been wondering for some time now why it was that you didn't see any of my reports until seven weeks ago. Can you tell me, or is it confidential?"

"It's not confidential; it's just a sad story," he said, his disappointment and regret registered in his face. "Chuck Talbet was a good employee for over twelve years. I liked him personally; he was a good man. About three years ago rumors about his son started floating through the executive suites. Apparently the kid had gotten tangled up in a very fast set. He was not only using drugs but had a very large balance on a credit line to some very unsavory people. To top it off, he gambled and signed notes, assuring his creditors that his father would pay.

"When it first came out, I offered Talbet a company loan to help out. He told me that the second mortgage on his house would take care of the accounts due and that his son was getting help. I had suggested he contact the police, but he indicated that his son's crowd wasn't the nicest and he had paid them off already. Not only would he then run the danger of prosecution, but there could be far-reaching repercussions on his family," Kevin explained, sick at heart.

"After a few weeks I didn't hear any more about it. And when I asked Chuck about his son, he said everything was under control. So I thought it was.

"The week before I asked you to come to New York, we had just finished settling on the lots for the computer research lab and the assembly factory with the board of directors. A couple of

questions had come up after the meeting, but
Chuck had already left. I told one of the directors I would investigate and get back to him.
When I called Talbet's office to get the answers I
wanted, he had gone for the day. So I asked his
secretary to bring me all his files on those projects. Needless to say, if he had been there, I
would never have seen your report. After I read
it—and it was good—I couldn't figure out why
Talbet hadn't gone with your proposals. So I
called his office back, just on a whim, and asked
for all your previous reports. All of them." His
voice was edged with anger.

"I was furious. I wanted to can him then and
there. Hobbs saved Talbet's rear end. He wisely
showed me that there could be extenuating circumstances and Talbet ought to get a chance to
explain his actions. Also, up until we found your
reports, there was no evidence that Chuck Talbet
hadn't been a loyal employee for a very long
time."

"Since you offered me the job, I take it Talbet
resigned when he realized he had been found
out," Jan concluded. Loathing the idea that all
her hard work had been hidden for Talbet's personal reasons, she had to agree that the man's
story was indeed sad and she felt sorry for him.

"The afternoon you left, Talbet came to my
office with his resignation," Kevin confirmed
with a nod. "He said, in a way, that he was glad
it was out in the open. When I asked him why
he'd done it, he told me that he had gone into

debt paying off his son's gambling notes. A real estate dealer from California had approached him with a land deal. If Talbet recommended the land, the dealer would alter the records and sell it for an inflated price and split the difference with Talbet. Chuck said the first few times he did it, it was easy because he needed the money so badly. Later, when his conscience returned, he was in too deep to quit."

"Poor guy. To work so hard all those years and end up with nothing."

"It's pathetic, isn't it," Kevin agreed. Then he tilted his head to one side in retrospect, and added, "Then again, you and I might never have met otherwise."

They had been leaning face-to-face over the back of the couch in his living room. He reached out and ran his fingers through the hair at her temple and stroked her cheekbone delicately with his thumb.

"You are the best thing that's ever happened to me, Jan. You fill up my life and give it a special purpose. I love you very much."

Kevin made loving sound so simple. *I love you.* Simple words. People used them all the time. They said them, they signed them on the bottoms of letters, they even engraved them in gold. But when Kevin said them, they seemed very real.

In all her life they had always been special, rare words. She knew Sybil and her grandfather loved her, but they weren't the type to say so.

She knew, too, that Caroline had loved her, but sisters assume it, they rarely say it. Jan always hoped her father loved her, but he had never once said so that she could remember. When Tony had said "I love you," it had been a lie.

But when Kevin said those simple words they implied so much more. They meant trust, affection, admiration, devotion, unselfish concern, acceptance, loyalty, passion. . . . They were written on his face and smoldered in his eyes.

Jan's vision clouded with emotion. Her heart raced and her throat tightened. She whispered, "I love being loved by you, Kevin. You are everything in the world I've ever wanted. I have so much love to give . . . and I want so much to give it all to you."

"But . . ." he prompted, misunderstanding her, his face a study of fear and apprehension.

"But nothing," she shot back, a small grin showing off her exquisite dimple. "If you'll just stand in one place long enough, I'll lavish it on you."

The concern was relieved and replaced with merriment on Kevin's lean, handsome features.

"You will, huh?" he teased. "I think I'd rather lie down and get comfortable before you get started."

Jan smiled slyly. "Stand, sit, lie down. Just let me know when you're ready."

Grabbing her hand and pulling her up from the couch and toward his bedroom, he moaned, "I'm ready! I've been ready all day!"

* * *

Kevin, propped up with pillows at his back, and Jan, her thighs still astride his hips, her head on his chest, were both reluctant to part from their union. A contented satisfaction had drugged them both.

"That was kind of like the words to that song you sang," he drawled absently. "What you said earlier about having so much to give."

Jan raised up to look blankly into his face, unsure of his meaning. Unselfconscious of her nudity, she braced her hands on his shoulders and waited for him to continue.

"The one about the stranger and you having more love to give than he would ever need," he explained.

"Yes, I guess so," she conceded.

"That night at Smitty's, did you sing that song for me?" He reached up and toyed with the rosy nipple of her breast and watched it grow hard again with his touch.

"I thought you had that figured out right away," she said as the now familiar quickening of her body signaled its arousal.

"I was hoping real hard," he admitted, moving to her other breast. "Is that why Simonson didn't want you to sing it?"

Consumed in her passion for him, Jan could only nod as her heart began to hammer and blood rushed through her veins.

"God. You respond so beautifully, so easily. I love watching your body respond to me and your eyes dilate and grow darker. You're like a wonderful, mysterious toy. I'm fascinated by all you can do and make me feel. It's amazing."

Jan groaned. "What's amazing is how much you talk sometimes," she said, scolding him as she arrested his lips with hers and turned his attention elsewhere.

The day after Jeff's operation was almost as trying as the day before. Jeff was awake for longer periods of time and more lucid, but his normally easygoing, shy disposition was testy and irritable from his discomfort. He would wake and be all right for nearly an hour before he would begin to whine and complain. He made everyone miserable for about a half hour before he would finally begin to complain of the pain in his hip and a throbbing ache in his leg. The nurse would bring him pain pills, and an hour later he would drop off to sleep. Jan and Kevin would sigh with relief, their patience and understanding severely taxed.

The cycle continued through most of the day. Evening came and, almost as if a cloud had been lifted, Jeff was suddenly more himself. He stayed awake longer and was irritable for a much shorter time. Although he still complained of pain, he was not frantic or beside himself from the discomfort.

The next forty-eight hours followed much the same pattern, with Jeff improving daily. Jan and Kevin spent their days entertaining Jeff and their nights entertaining each other.

On the third day Kevin arrived from the office

just as Jeff was settling down for a nap after an exhausting morning in physical therapy learning how to walk with the awkward crutches.

Kevin and Jan decided to go down to the cafeteria for coffee. Returning an hour later, Jan stopped dead in her tracks outside Jeff's door as familiar voices came from Jeff's room.

"I know you," came Jeff's high-pitched young voice. "You're my grampa. My mommy's daddy."

"Ah, yes . . . I am," came the deeper, astonished voice of Jeff Manning.

"I know you because my aunt Jan keeps your picture on the mantel at home." Jeff seemed to sense the older man's confusion at his knowing his identity and went on to explain. "She tells me and Tommy about you and her mommy a lot. And about my mommy and daddy."

"Ah . . . may . . . I ask what she says about me?" Manning faltered, obviously nervous.

"Sure," said Jeff enthusiastically. "She says you are a very nice man. My aunt Jan tells good stories about going to the amusement park with you and her mommy before my mommy was even born. She has pictures of it and shows us them." He paused, then continued. "She says you would probably come visit, but you run a very big company and you go far away a lot and you don't have a lot of extra time. She said maybe when you retire someday you might come see us. Are you retired now?"

"No, Jeff, I'm not retired. In fact . . . I guess you could say I'm just starting. You see, son, I . . . I've made some terrible mistakes in my life

—done some awful things. I'm here to make things right, if it's not too late."

In the hall Kevin had been holding Jan, his arms wrapped tightly, supportingly, around her from behind. His chin resting on her head, he could feel the tension in her muscles and the quaking that came from deep inside her, but he could not see the tears gliding down her pale face.

"I know about making dumb mistakes." Jeff was empathetic. "They're a lot worse if you keep them secret and don't tell the truth," he said, referring to his own guilt over Mrs. Silverman's begonias.

"I think you're right, Jeff," agreed the older Jeff. "Tell me, son, do you miss your mother?"

"Sometimes," Jeff said thoughtfully. "I don't remember her very well, but I think I do because of the stories Aunt Jan and Sybil tell about her. They say Tommy is a lot like her and my daddy and I'm more like you and Aunt Jan."

"How is that?"

"I keep things inside. Aunt Jan says she does, too, and it's okay, but sometimes you have to speak up or no one will hear you and then you won't get what you really want." He paused again, as if remembering. "That's true too. Lots of times Tommy talks so fast I end up eating those chocolate nutty things he likes when I would rather have a banana split."

There was a short silence in the room. Out in the hall Jan hung her head in remorse for the banana splits as she listened to her father talking to her dead sister's son so intimately, more confidentially than he had every spoken to either Caroline or herself.

"Your aunt Jan is a very wise woman, Jeff," came the old man's voice. "And I think that's a problem I have too." He stopped, hesitant to go on. "The mess my life is in right now is because I couldn't or wouldn't say what was on my mind or in my heart. Especially to the people I cared most about."

"I know about that too," Jeff stated in a very adult manner. "Sybil says that sometimes, when we don't think about what we do, we hurt the people we love most. She says that lots of times when we're angry or sad we try to make the people closest to us angry and sad, too, because we don't want to feel that way alone. Sybil says that the people who love us don't really mind it when you do it. They might be mad or hurt, but they forgive you right away because they love you no matter what you do."

"You make it sound so simple," murmured the older Jeff, wishing it were.

"It is that simple," came a female voice from the doorway.

Both Jeffs turned to see the tear-stained Jan standing in the doorway, Kevin by her side. Her eyes held a lifetime of hope; her lips quivered as she attempted a small smile of encouragement.

Jeff Manning studied his daughter hopefully. After an eternity he got up slowly from his chair and extended his arms to Jan in a time-honored gesture of loving welcome.

Her first step was hesitant, remembering past rebukes. The next six or seven steps she took swiftly, as if afraid the arms would close again and she would miss her chance.

Jeff Manning folded his daughter into an awkward embrace. They held each other for several seconds before Manning took his little girl's face between his hands and looked deep into her eyes, his wife's eyes, for the love and forgiveness young Jeff had spoken of.

"*Can* you forgive me for all the pain I've caused you? For the pain I let Caroline take to her grave? For neglecting the two of you and my grandchildren? Is there enough forgiveness anywhere to cover all I've done wrong?" he asked, his voice cracking.

Silently Jan nodded slowly before she softly whispered, "I love you, Daddy."

The old man's eyes closed in relief and profound gratitude and humility. Then he pulled his daughter into a tight, natural embrace and in a hoarse voice uttered, "I love you too, baby. More than anything."

Later that afternoon Hobbs arrived to find the foursome bidding a cheerful farewell to Steve, whose parents had come to take him home.

The two older men were introduced. Hobbs, being the observant and wise old man that he was, sensed Manning's presence there was an auspicious occasion. He watched Kevin turn a leery eye toward Jeff Manning and stood protectively close to Jan. Jan sent glances full of awe and admiration to her father as he became acquainted with his grandson.

Tactfully he mentioned that he had been to Kevin's apartment and prepared dinner and that there was more than enough for three. He went on to add that he would be most pleased to stay and try to entertain young Jeffrey for the evening if the others would care to go for a bite to eat.

At his apartment Kevin sat quietly and listened patiently while Jeff Manning and his daughter made a valiant effort to close at least part of the gap between them. Kevin had tried to excuse himself from this very personal reunion, but both parties involved had asked him to stay, one out of respect for him, the other out of love.

Reluctantly Kevin had to admire the old man. He could only guess how much courage and desperation had driven him to humble himself before his daughter and to beg her forgiveness.

As for Jan, he was again amazed and proud of her deep and overflowing capacity to love and, in this case, forgive so completely. There was no trace of condemnation or bitterness for her father's actions toward herself or Caroline. Only hope that this was just the first of many close personal communes with her father. She actually glowed in her contentment. She was a remarkably loving woman. And she was his.

Much later that night two lovers lay sated with their bodies entwined, clinging to each other.

"Mmm," Jan hummed as Kevin moved his

hand over her back in a slow circular motion. "I'm half afraid I'm going to wake up and find I've been living in a dream. I can't remember ever being so completely and totally happy before."

"I was that good for you," Kevin retorted, sounding very proud of himself, purposely misinterpreting her comment.

Jan giggled softly against his chest. "Yes, you were," she stated, "and add to that everything I've always wanted and you have a very content woman."

"List the things you've always wanted . . . in order of priority," he instructed, curious.

There was a moment of reflection before she complied. "A good man to love. A wonderful man to love me. Children to love and care for. My father's love. A new apartment. An interesting job with a challenge. Those are the big ones. Do you want the little ones, too?"

Baffled, he skipped her question and asked his own. "What new apartment? Are you going to take an apartment in Denver? Are you tired of commuting from the cabin?"

"No. I want a new apartment here in New York. This one is way too small for all of us."

Kevin pushed her away so that he could look her full in the face. Leaning on one elbow and scowling in confusion, he stared down at her and stammered, "This one? . . . For all of us?"

Inhaling anxiously, Jan rattled off, "Well, if Hobbs stays with us, and I hope he does, where will the boys sleep? Then, of course, there's that rug in the living room. No one in their right mind with children would have wheat-colored carpets. And we'd have to hire a full-time house-keeper just to keep the fingerprints off the windows. And you realize, of course, Baby is part of the package. Black Bart is Sybil's dog, so he'll stay in Colorado. Does this building allow pets?"

When he answered her question with silence, she went on in a rush. "Then we'll need to consider schools and playgrounds and parks. And . . ."

"What exactly are you telling me, Jan?" Kevin interrupted.

Jan's heart was pounding with fear. Maybe she had assumed too much. She forged on. "Well, the boys and I discussed coming to New York and living here permanently—with you . . . if you'll have us," she finished nervously.

There was total quiet for several minutes before Kevin spoke. Jan was very close to death.

"Let me get this straight. Before you even left Colorado, you and the boys decided to come live in New York with me, even though you knew there was a good chance you might have to face your father."

"Yes," she whispered.

"You planned to give up your business and home . . . your whole life to come here to be with me."

"Yes," she repeated.

"That's your big surprise?"

"Yes."

The moss-green eyes were large and anxious

and full of love. Her lips were still rosy and swollen. Her skin remained flushed from their loving.

Kevin adored her. "Every time I'm sure I can't love you more than I do, you do something like this and my love increases a thousandfold. I don't know how I contain it all. You just keep filling me full of your unselfishness, and I'm always surprised I don't burst wide open. I feel like I will, but I don't. Jan, I love you so very much," he marveled. "What am I going to do without you?"

Jan's rising hopes and exaltation were dashed to the ground. "Without me?" she repeated, mystified.

"I'm leaving New York, sweetheart. As of September first I won't be living here anymore. The fact that you are willing to give up everything to be with me is overwhelming. I can't tell you how much it will always mean to me," he said solemnly, leading her on.

"But where? When . . . I . . . why?" she muttered. She could feel tears welling in her eyes. Kevin didn't love her enough to marry her. She'd thrown herself and the boys at him and he'd taken a smooth sidestep to avoid a direct hit. She was still in his bed, naked. It was all too humiliating and painful.

Reading her every thought, Kevin was ashamed of his game. "Jan, please don't move to New York. Stay in Colorado. Marry me. Be my wife. Let me love you forever. Have my babies. Allow me to love and care for Tommy and Jeff," he said, punctuating his speech with tiny kisses across her face.

Totally lost, Jan searched his face.

"My beautiful, wonderful, adorable Jan. You can't move to New York, because I'm moving to Denver. Well, the company headquarters are moving to Denver. I had my heart set on a cabin near Pleasant Valley, with a pond and a ridiculous waterfall in the backyard," he concluded, grinning from ear to ear, thrilled by her telling reaction to his announcement.

Jan simply raised her arms up around his neck and pulled him forward. The threatening tears spilled over onto her cheeks in joy.

After several minutes Kevin pulled away to wallow in the happiness shining in her eyes, her gorgeous eyes. He leaned down and kissed a tear off her cheek.

"I take it you like my surprise," he stated mundanely.

"I'm crazy about it." Her dimple sparkled as she smiled ecstatically.

Kevin kissed her and asked archly, "What's Jeff going to say when he finds out you let the cat out of the bag?"

"Oh. Well," she said offhandedly, "we'll just have to reenact the scene tomorrow. Dressed and out of bed, of course. And you'll have to look extremely surprised before you spring your own surprise."

"Will he let me kiss you?" he asked, considering the proposal.

"Well, I did warn him that you might. He

would probably be very disappointed if you didn't. He said kissing and surprises sort of go together," she explained.

"Smart boy. Okay, we'll clean up our surprise act and take it to the hospital tomorrow for a grand one-time performance. But I think we ought to do a little rehearsing tonight, first."

"Oh," she murmured, smiling knowingly. "Which part do you need to brush up on?"

"I think we should get all that surprised kissing down pat. We don't want to disappoint a child, do we?"

"You and your excuses," she chided him.

They kissed well into the night, and a clever Kevin used the same excuse twice more in the early morning. Later they got rave reviews on their performance.

The End?

The end of a book is never really *the end* for a person who reads. He or she can always open another. And another.

Every page holds possibilities.

But millions of kids don't see them. Don't know they're there. Millions of kids can't read, or won't.

That's why there's RIF. Reading is Fundamental (RIF) is a national nonprofit program that works with thousands of community organizations to help young people discover the fun—and the importance—of reading.

RIF motivates kids so that they *want* to read. And RIF works directly with parents to help them encourage their children's reading. RIF gets books to children and children into books, so they grow up reading and become adults who can read. Adults like you.

For more information on how to start a RIF program in your neighborhood, or help your own child grow up reading, write to:

RIF
Dept. BK-1
Box 23444
Washington, D.C.
20026

Founded in 1966, RIF is a national non-profit organization with local projects run by volunteers in every state of the union.

LOOK FOR THESE TITLES FROM PAGEANT BOOKS!

A CASE FOR LOVE
Paula Williams

Tracey Moran's latest case looks routine enough, until she discovers that her opposing counsel is the notorious Jed Davis, an attorney whose brash good looks are as engaging as his courtroom battles. In his arms Tracey wonders if it is too late to keep her heart from overruling her head. By the author of *LOVESONG*, available from Pageant Books.

ISBN: 0-517-00641-3   Price: $2.50

MY ENEMY, MY LOVE
Mary Ann Taylor

As opponents in a struggle to develop a choice piece of California waterfront, Sassy Dale and Mark Stewart lock horns. Are Mark's romantic intentions for real, or a clever ploy to undermine the opposition? And can Sassy, whose heart pounds whenever Mark is near, convince him that the seaside resort is as precious as the love they share?

ISBN: 0-517-00075-X   Price: $2.50

PARADISE DAYS, PARADISE NIGHTS
Alyssa Douglas

Samantha Huxley is a tough insurance investigator on assignment at a lush Caribbean resort. When her heart is turned by the very man she's supposed to be investigating, Samantha learns the hard way about mixing business with pleasure!

ISBN: 0-517-00007-5   Price: $2.50

ON SALE NOW!

ADD A PAGEANT ROMANCE
TO YOUR LIFE!

LOVE'S MEMORIES

Their youthful passions were savagely swept away by their angry parents, who had their marriage annulled. But Marikka is destined to become reacquainted with Senator Jordan Ferrell—a meeting as exhilarating and intoxicating as their reborn love. Will their future burn brightly or are they fated to lose everything again?

By Heidi Strasser

ISBN: 0-517-00669-3   Price: $2.50

DECEIVE ME, DARLING

When Cathlyn and Marc collide trying to hail a cab during a Chicago snowstorm, they end up sharing more than a ride. But soon Cathlyn realizes that Marc is hiding something from her. Will his secretiveness tarnish the love and moments of shared rapture? Is he her knight in shining armor or merely an imposter? Cathlyn will stop at nothing to win this handsome and passionate man.

By Barbara Siddon

ISBN: 0-517-00079-2   Price: $2.50

CONTEMPORARY
CLASSICS

ON SALE NOW!